Gian... ...u might
not want this situation but you want
me, as much... I want you.'

...m
...ch
...op,
...his
...w.
...get
...p.'

...id
...ng

...ng
...'m

...ser,
...are
...But

...han
...ona
...urs,
...r to

THE CHATSFIELD

SERIES 2

Maisey Yates
SHEIKH'S DESERT DUTY

Abby Green
DELUCCA'S MARRIAGE CONTRACT

Carol Marinelli
PRINCESS'S SECRET BABY

Kate Hewitt
VIRGIN'S SWEET REBELLION

Caitlin Crews
GREEK'S LAST REDEMPTION

Michelle Conder
RUSSIAN'S RUTHLESS DEMAND

Susanna Carr
TYCOON'S DELICIOUS DEBT

Melanie Milburne
BILLIONAIRE'S ULTIMATE ACQUISITION

8 volumes to collect—
you won't want to miss out!

The world's most elite hotel is looking for a jewel in its crown and Spencer Chatsfield has found it. But Isabella Harrington, the girl from his past, refuses to sell!

Now the world's most decadent destinations have become a chessboard in this game of power, passion and pleasure...

Welcome to

THE

CHATSFIELD

Synonymous with style, sensation...and scandal!

With the eight Chatsfield siblings happily married and settling down, it's time for a new generation of Chatsfields to shine!

Spencer Chatsfield steps in as CEO, determined to prove his worth. But when he approaches Isabella Harrington of Harringtons Boutique hotels with the offer of a merger that would benefit them both... he's left with a stinging red palm-shaped mark on his cheek!

And so begins a game of cat and mouse that will shape the future of the Chatsfields and the Harringtons for ever.

But neither knows that there's one stakeholder with the power to decide their fate...and that person's identity will shock both the Harringtons *and* the Chatsfields.

Just who will come out on top?

DELUCCA'S MARRIAGE CONTRACT

BY
ABBY GREEN

Harrington Family Tree

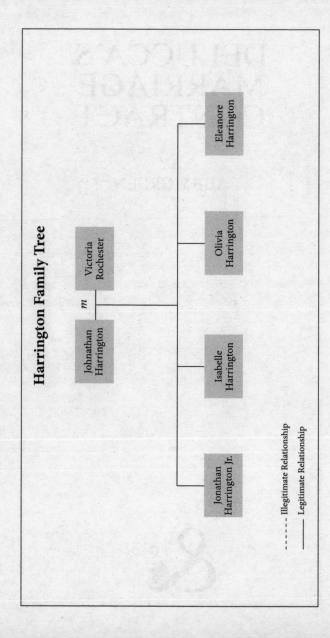

Johnathan Harrington *m* Victoria Rochester

Jonathan Harrington Jr.   Isabelle Harrington   Olivia Harrington   Eleanore Harrington

- - - - - Illegitimate Relationship

——— Legitimate Relationship

Chatsfield Family Tree

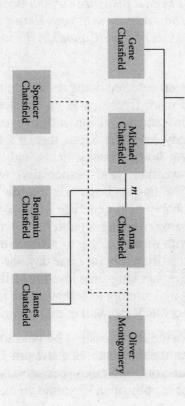

Gene Chatsfield

Spencer Chatsfield

Michael Chatsfield

m

Benjamin Chatsfield

James Chatsfield

Anna Chatsfield

Oliver Montgomery

This is for Paul Gallant, my Canadian pen pal since we worked waiting tables together in Dublin's Temple Bar (pre stag/hen party era) in 1990. It's been a pleasure communicating in the old-fashioned way with you. Here's to many more years of Irish/Canadian dispatches. x

Abby Green deferred doing a social anthropology degree to work freelance as an assistant director in the film and television industry—which is a social study in itself! Since then it's been early starts, long hours, mucky fields, ugly car parks and wet-weather gear—especially working in Ireland. She has no bona fide qualifications, but could probably help negotiate a peace agreement between two warring countries after years of dealing with recalcitrant actors. Since discovering a guide to writing romance one day, she decided to capitalise on her long-time love for Mills & Boon® romances and attempt to follow in the footsteps of such authors as Kate Walker and Penny Jordan.

She's enjoying the excuse to be paid to sit inside, away from the elements. She lives in Dublin and hopes that you will enjoy her stories. You can e-mail her at abbygreen3@yahoo.co.uk.

PROLOGUE

'THAT'S THE DEAL, Delucca, take it or leave it. I don't think I need to tell you that if you leave it the O'Connor brand won't be affected.'

Giancarlo Delucca gritted his jaw at the arrogant tone. The unspoken insinuation from the older Irish man wasn't subtle: *But the Delucca brand might languish in European shopping aisles for years before making it globally.*

Gianni, still reeling slightly, looked at Liam O'Connor, who sat in a leather chair with his back to the impressive view of Dublin's financial district.

'And what does your daughter think of this proposed arranged marriage?'

O'Connor's grey eyes narrowed, and there was a barely perceptible tightening around his mouth. 'Keelin is loyal to the family business.'

Gianni responded with a hint of incredulity.

'Loyal enough to agree to a marriage of convenience?'

Suddenly feeling agitated, Gianni didn't wait for a reply and went to stand at one of the huge floor-to-ceiling windows. He put his hands in his pockets to stop himself from running them impatiently through his hair—a bad habit. He felt claustrophobic. *Marriage.* That word called up all sorts of dark images and bad memories. He'd only ever seen the worst a marriage had to offer so he'd vowed never to take that route himself. But the unpalatable fact was that he needed this merger with the vastly successful O'Connor Foods brand to break into the more lucrative global market, and namely, America.

That would take him away from the bitter memories of his childhood and young adulthood. It would civilise the Delucca name, make him invulnerable, and in time no one would ever remember that *Delucca* had once been one of the Mafia's most notorious names.

O'Connor's voice came from behind him. 'Keelin is a beautiful woman. Well educated. She'll be an asset on your arm as you move forward and expand.'

Gianni's mouth tightened as the kind of domestic scenario he hadn't ever envisaged took root in his mind, much to his disgust. He didn't want O'Connor to see the myriad emotions he was feeling in his eyes, so didn't turn around. 'You think that I can't find a wife of my own choosing?' Not that he'd contemplated it!

Liam O'Connor laughed dryly. 'Delucca, I have no doubt that you could click your fingers and find a wife in seconds. Your reputation—'

Gianni swung around then, cutting the other man off. He forced his voice to sound calm when inside he felt hot, irritated. 'Be very careful, O'Connor.'

The other man stood up from behind his desk and came around it. He was tall and imposing. Handsome, with a head of thick silver hair. The older alpha male squaring up to the younger one, even if Gianni was taller, younger and infinitely more handsome than O'Connor ever had been. Gianni knew all about alpha males; he'd squared up to the most alpha of them all: his father.

O'Connor spoke bluntly. 'No other company can give you the instant sheen of respectability that we can, merely by association. If we merge, people trust our name enough to automatically trust you. Your products will be on shelves across the world within months. I am offering you the chance to prove your commitment to both your brand and your family name. You don't need me to tell you that the people you will be dealing with will be more likely to put their trust and investment in a family man.'

Again the unspoken rang as loudly as a bell in the room: *And in someone who didn't have links to the underworld, or who had the damaging reputation of a playboy.* Damn him. O'Connor was right. So how badly did he want this? Badly enough to embark on a union he'd never wished for? For the sake of a deal? Social acceptance? Professional respectability?

But it's the deal of a lifetime, whispered a little voice.

Wanting to assert his position more, Gianni pointed out, 'That may very well be the case but don't forget that your own business will be reinvigorated by a new association with a luxury Italian brand of products, the first merger of its kind.'

O'Connor inclined his head with a spark in his eyes. He obviously didn't like to be reminded that his motives weren't exactly altruistic.

And then Gianni asked abruptly, 'Why is it so important to you that marriage to your daughter is part of the deal?'

The spark in O'Connor's eyes was quickly veiled as he said easily, 'She's our only child and heir. I'm an old-fashioned man, Delucca. I want her future to be secure, and through her and you, we keep our name alive.'

Gianni felt a niggle of suspicion but then something caught his peripheral vision and he looked past O'Connor to where a group of framed photos were hung on a wall. He walked over. There were pictures of O'Connor with various celebrities, including two American presidents, and then presumably his wife—an attractive woman with strawberry blonde hair and green eyes.

And below them all was an image of a young woman on a horse, head back and wide generous mouth open, clearly laughing. Slim shoulders. A snug T-shirt hugged generous firm breasts. He could just make out a narrow waist, gently flaring hips. Taut thighs. She was stunningly beautiful. Almond-shaped green eyes, lighter than her mother's. Vibrant red hair pulled back into a messy ponytail. Pale skin with flushed rosy cheeks. Freckles.

Something deep in Gianni's gut clenched at her unadorned beauty. Even though she wasn't remotely his type.

He barely picked up on the faintly smug tone in O'Connor's voice when the man said, 'That's my daughter, Keelin. So have you come to a decision?'

Gianni didn't answer out loud. He didn't need to. They both knew the answer.

CHAPTER ONE

KEELIN O'CONNOR SURVEYED the lavishly decorated hotel room in the exclusive Harrington Hotel in Rome. Almost nothing was visible because glossy shopping bags covered every surface. As a shopping novice, she hoped she'd gone far enough, not really knowing what constituted gross levels of consumerism beyond what she saw on some trashy reality-TV programmes of the rich and famous.

Her *fiancé*—who also happened to be a complete stranger—was due any minute and she hated that the palms of her hands were sweaty with nerves when her blood still boiled with anger and humiliation at what her father expected her to do.

'You can't be serious.' She'd looked at her father two weeks ago and battled a very familiar sense of angry futility.

Liam O'Connor's expression was as hard as flint. 'I am.'

Keelin had spoken slowly as if to make sure she wasn't in the middle of a nightmare. 'You've sold me off in some marriage deal to a complete stranger—'

Her father slashed a hand through the air. 'It is *not* like that. Giancarlo Delucca is one of Italy's most innovative entrepreneurs. Italian food and wine exports are booming and in the space of only three years the Delucca name has gained respect all over Europe, not to mention tripled its profits, which is unheard of at the moment.'

'So what the hell does that have to do with me?'

Her tall father had put his hands on his desk and leant forward. 'What it has to do with you, my girl, is *everything*. I want a merger with this man to secure the future of O'Connor Foods and as my daughter you are part of the deal.'

Keelin's hands curled to fists but she'd barely noticed her nails digging into soft skin. 'This is archaic.'

Her father straightened up and said scathingly, 'Don't be so naive. This is about business. Giancarlo Delucca is a young man, and good-looking. Rich. Any woman would be delighted to have him as her husband.'

Keelin had responded bitterly. 'Any woman, perhaps, with about two brain cells to rub together.' She'd ignored her father's darkening expression and tried to call up the little she knew of Delucca from her overheated brain. 'Doesn't he have links to the Mafia?'

Her father replied tautly. 'His *father* had links to the Mafia. And he's dead. That's all in the past now. Delucca is determined to put it behind him and prove to people that he's respectable. That's why he's willing to marry and settle down.'

Keelin laughed but it sounded strangled and semi-hysterical. 'Lucky me!'

Liam O'Connor's grey gaze, so different to Keelin's own green one, narrowed on her. 'Haven't you always wanted me to involve you in the business?'

'Yes,' she'd said huskily, emotion a tight ball in her chest to be reminded of how comprehensively she'd been shut out. 'But as the person who stands to inherit the O'Connor brand. Not as some chattel to be sold off to the highest bidder.'

Her father's mouth had tightened. 'You've hardly given me the confidence that you can be trusted to inherit anything, Keelin.'

Futile anger rose in a dizzying rush and, terrified emotion might leak out of her eyes, she'd stalked over to the large window which showcased an impressive view of a soaring modern bridge, named after the great playwright Samuel Beckett, over the River Liffey. Dublin had sparkled benignly in the spring sunshine.

But she'd seen none of it. She'd felt only an inner tsunami of pain to be so misunderstood, *still*. She'd known for ever that she was a disappointment to her parents: to her mother for not being the girlie girl she wanted to show off. And to her father for being a girl, and not a worthier boy. And as soon as Keelin had recognised that as a distinct lack of love, it had seared a need into her psyche to get her father's attention at all costs, which had manifested in a series of teenage rebellions that had been as futile as they were excruciating to remember now.

And even though she'd matured and left those petty rebellions behind, nothing had really changed. Her parents hadn't even deigned to come and see her graduate from university recently.

Her own reflection was distorted in the glass—pale face, huge eyes. Red hair. Too red. It had always marked her out as far too easy to pinpoint when there was trouble, unwittingly helping her to act out her pathetic bid for love and attention.

When she'd felt composed enough she'd turned around again. 'And what about our name? If I marry him it'll die out anyway!'

Her father had shaken his head. 'No, it won't.

Delucca has agreed that our name and branding will remain and be passed down to your sons.'

Her sons. With a complete stranger. A gangster.

Her father had walked around the desk to come and stand a few feet away from her, his face softening slightly. Emotion had gripped her again. Was she such a sucker for any sliver of affection that she would fall for this thinly veiled act?

He'd sighed heavily. 'The truth is that O'Connor Foods is struggling, like almost every other business out there.'

Keelin had frowned; she'd been aware that the company hadn't been doing as well as in previous years but not badly enough to merit alarm. And how would she really know when she was kept firmly excluded from the inner sanctum? 'Struggling—how do you mean?'

He'd waved a hand, avoiding a direct answer. 'Aligning with Delucca will give us the boost we need, and the protection, going forward. And then there's you. I want to know that your future is secured.'

Keelin hadn't been fooled for a second that he genuinely cared for her welfare even though a weak part of her yearned for it. She'd taken advantage of his softer stance to try to make him see that she was serious about wanting to be involved. 'But my future *will* be secure. I can work with you to help shore up the defences, take the company forward. I'm ready to—'

He'd lifted a hand, any trace of softness disappearing. 'If you truly want to prove that you can be part of this company in a meaningful way, then this marriage is the only solution, Keelin.'

A tiny flame of hope sputtered out. It mocked the defences she thought she'd honed over years of neglect. She shook her head, a sense of betrayal rising within her. 'I won't do it.'

Her father lashed back angrily. 'I should have known you'd balk when it came to proving the depth of your loyalty. If you walk away from this, you can consider yourself on your own.'

For a moment she'd felt as if he'd punched her in the softest part of her belly. All she wanted was to show her loyalty to her family legacy, and she was finally being offered a chance but in exchange for her personal freedom.

She'd felt sick to think that it had come to this—the ultimate rejection, if she said no. But then, in a blinding flash of inspiration, a scenario had taken shape. A burgeoning sense of hope had filled her as she said slowly, 'What if we meet and Delucca doesn't want to marry me?'

Her father waved a hand dismissively. 'Of course he'll want to marry you. You're a beautiful young woman, and you're bringing with you the opportunity he needs to break into the global market. He won't let that slip away.'

But Keelin had been barely listening to her father any more, her heart palpitating at the thought of a way out of this crazy scenario without having to burn her bridges entirely. So she'd agreed to meet with Delucca and here she was now, seconds away from that meeting.

She'd exhaustively researched him in the meantime and found that clearly he was obsessed with proving that the persistent rumour of links to the Mafia were just that. In every interview he put the focus on his business concerns and moving forward. He was the epitome of casual Italian elegance, and to Keelin's chagrin she hadn't been able to repress a shiver of awareness when she'd seen his photos. He was darkly gorgeous, masculine. An air of intensity about him. And also danger.

He seemed hell-bent on proving himself to be a million miles removed from the scandals of his father's life, a man who had been brutally murdered by a rival Mafia faction.

And when it came to lovers he was never pictured with the same stunning woman more than twice. They were all of the same ilk: tall, brunette, sleek and gorgeous. Discreet, and oozing effortless classy style. Which was in keeping with his apparent bid not to draw adverse attention to himself. True, he skirted on the edges of being known as a playboy, but was never photographed behaving badly. And there were no salacious kiss-and-tell stories. So the playboy moniker was pretty benign.

Evidently he didn't let women get in his way when it came to his ruthless ambition. And respectability and discretion were important to him. So this gave Keelin all the ammunition she needed. A man like that couldn't want a wife! And she'd decided she needed to make herself over into everything that might possibly repel him from this union.

She'd ended up with an over-the-top trashy caricature of the kind of girl she'd known in her school peer group: rich, privileged, shallow, vain. And hopefully the kind of woman someone like Giancarlo Delucca would run screaming from.

She checked herself now in a nearby mirror— dress: *short*; long red hair: *big*; make-up: *a lot*. She made a face. Her mother would approve wholeheartedly. She spritzed more perfume on, swallowing back a sneeze at the overwhelming fumes.

A peremptory knock came to the hotel room door and Keelin's belly swooped alarmingly. She wasn't ready for this, she felt ridiculous. He'd see through her in an instant.

The knock came again, a little sharper. She steeled herself. She had to be ready. This was a fight for her independence and future.

Fixing what she hoped was a bright vacuous smile on her face she walked to the door and opened it. But the smile faltered when she had to lift her eyeline to the hunk in the dark blue suit on the other side.

One thing got through to her shocked brain: no mere picture could have prepared her for Giancarlo Delucca in the flesh.

Gianni reeled as he tried to take in the woman before him and not suffocate with the wave of noxious perfume that had enveloped him as soon as she'd opened the door.

His first impression was *excess* and everything in him recoiled from it. Lots of vibrant red hair, lots of make-up and a tight sleeveless bandeau dress that was eye-wateringly short, showing off acres of suspiciously tanned-looking skin, and an abundant amount of equally faux-tanned cleavage.

The woman in front of him didn't remotely resemble the picture he'd seen in O'Connor's office. Anger pierced him to think he'd been deceived. And rendered speechless for a moment, a state he was *not* used to, they just stared at each other.

And then the perfume seemed to dissipate mercifully, bringing some oxygen to his brain, restoring his faculties. He pushed the anger down, telling himself he was being too hasty.

Just as he thought that, he saw the gold necklace nestling close to that upsurge of cleavage. Joined-together looping letters spelled out *K-e-e-l-i-n*. Diamonds twinkled from either end.

His last lover had favoured nothing more obvious than tiny diamond stud earrings. But he forced himself to look at his potential future wife, smile and say smoothly, 'Miss O'Connor, it's a pleasure to meet you. I'm Giancarlo Delucca, welcome to Italy.'

She blinked, smiled and stepped back. 'Please excuse me. I just got back from doing some shopping near the Via del Corso.'

Gianni walked into the room, aware that even though she was in spindly high heels, she'd be tall without them. About five foot eight, he guessed. A dart of awareness pierced him, surprising him.

He heard the door click behind him and he had the most bizarre urge to turn around and escape. *Fast.* He pushed it down. He'd agreed to this cold-blooded agreement for lots of reasons, but also because he'd decided that he could handle a marriage that was a business transaction, not an emotional or romantic endeavour.

He steeled himself and turned to face Keelin again. For a second something about her over-the-top look felt slightly *off* but he got distracted by those unbelievably long legs and that impressive cleavage. *Dio.* He'd expected fresh-faced natural beauty. An intelligent refined woman, not a tarted-up society girl.

Keelin waved an arm to indicate the hundreds of luxe bags and gushed, 'Thank you so much for the welcome gift of the credit card, *such* a thoughtful gesture. Shopping in Rome is my absolute favourite. It's made me feel right at home.'

She glanced up from under her lashes in a way that set his teeth on edge, even as he realised that under all that smoky eye make-up her eyes were as huge and stunning as he might have expected. A kind of mossy green he'd never seen before.

'I'm afraid I saw the word *trousseau* and I got a little excited. They're delivering the rest tomorrow.'

'The rest?' He blanched at that, eyes widening slightly.

'Oh, yes.' She trilled a little laugh. 'This is just a few things to keep me going.

'Actually—' she looked around speculatively and bit her lip '—the Harrington Hotel is a beautiful hotel, Mr Delucca, but I'm used to a little more space. At The Chatsfield, for instance, they're so wonderful about storing shopping.'

Gianni bit down the distaste—he'd chosen this hotel because of its hushed discreet exclusivity. The Chatsfield's opulent luxuriousness tended to attract more attention, which Gianni instinctively shied away from.

'Anyway,' Keelin said brightly, drawing Gianni's attention back to her, 'this is fine for now, and I just heard a rumour that Sheikh Zayn and Sophie Parsons might be staying here.' She rolled her eyes theatrically. 'Did you see the pictures of their wedding? *So* glamorous and romantic. I'd love to catch a glimpse of them.'

No, Gianni thought grimly. He hadn't seen pictures of some society wedding. However, it rang a bell and he did recall something now about James Chatsfield hitting the headlines again for living up to his playboy reputation in some exclusive ski resort, which was just another reason to prefer the discretion of The Harrington.

Keelin was smiling at him guilelessly. She looked sweet but vacant. And for the first time Gianni felt something inside him tighten in rejection of a wife who would be little more than a glossy appendage on the end of his arm. Even though that's what he'd told himself he'd be happy with for the sake of a deal.

Before he could formulate another sentence though, Keelin had moved over to a small table with an ice bucket on top. As she bent forward slightly Gianni couldn't help but let his eyes follow the lean lines of her body. She was slim and toned, yet as undeniably curvy as she'd been in the photo. That at least hadn't lied.

The swell of her breast against the taut material of the dress made heat pulse in his groin. It confounded him. His head rejected everything about this woman but his body was running to a different beat. A much more visceral one.

Keelin was pouring the sparkling golden liquid into a glass. She turned back to him and said brightly, 'Champers?'

Gianni noticed that she had full lips and the slightest overbite, an anomaly that made him think of carnal things, like how her mouth would look wrapped around—

'I *love* champagne, a little weakness of mine, I'm afraid.'

She was thrusting a full glass at him and breaking apart the completely unwelcome X-rated image before he could respond. Gianni took it and watched as she turned to put the bottle back, the tight black sheath of her designer dress stretching over those curves again, teasing him.

When she turned back, his eyes tracked to her

breasts and she caught him looking, but before he could lambast himself for this completely un-suave behaviour, she was saying excitedly, 'Do you like the look? I *love* Italian designers.'

She held up her glass and smiled brightly. 'Cheers, Mr Delucca.'

Gianni forced down the sense of things veering out of his control to see that wide smile caked in so much lipstick. He held up his glass too. He would not be deterred by some bad taste and heavy make-up. Or by the fact that the photo he'd seen must have been taken when she was sixteen.

All this woman needed was a little finessing. He would hire an expert stylist to make her over. Already he was imagining what she might look like without that dreadful tan job and make-up. In a dress that flowed over her curves.

He felt as if some measure of control was returning for the first time since she'd opened the suite door. He smiled. 'Please call me Gianni.'

For a second he thought he saw a flash of something like panic in those huge eyes but it disappeared and she frowned, a small line marring the otherwise smooth perfection of her forehead. 'But isn't your name Giancarlo?'

Her Irish accent mangled his name charmingly. 'I prefer Gianni.'

She shrugged and smiled before throwing

back at least half a glass of the champagne in one go. 'Gianni, it is then.'

She reached for the bottle again to refill her glass and a memory of his drunk father exploded into his head. Angry and unsettled at that intrusive and unwelcome image because it reminded him of so much more, Gianni put his glass down on a nearby table.

She looked at him, surprised, and he said abruptly, 'I'm afraid I can't indulge. I just came to see how you were settling in. Needless to say we have lots to talk about.'

She looked at him blankly for a moment before what he said seemed to register and then she let out a slightly embarrassed giggle. 'Oh, you mean the *wedding*. Of course, silly me. Yes, *lots* to talk about.'

She threw back more champagne and the action alternately annoyed and aroused him. His recent sense of being in control eroding slightly. 'We'll meet downstairs in the bar at seven-thirty?'

She nodded enthusiastically. 'Fab, can't wait.'

Gianni pulled a card out of his inside pocket and handed it to her; for a moment she did that blank thing again before taking it.

He quashed the flash of irritation and explained, 'Those are my private numbers in case you need to contact me in the meantime.'

She looked at him and smiled and for a second lust rose again to drown out all of the very mixed things Gianni was feeling. This meeting had definitely been surreal and disturbing in a way he hadn't expected.

He backed away, determined not to allow the sense of disappointment to rise. 'Till later, Keelin. I look forward to getting to know you.' He had to quash the uncharitable thought that there wasn't much more *to* know.

She tipped her glass towards him and some champagne sloshed out onto the stunning carpet but she was oblivious. *'Ciao.'* She giggled, 'See? I'm already practically fluent.'

Gianni smiled but it was hard. He let himself out of the suite and took the lift back to the lobby and strode back out to this waiting car. The sense of relief was enormous. But he refused to be dissuaded by the fact that his evidently not very bright fiancée had apparently spent what looked to him to be the national debt of a small country in the space of a few hours. He'd given her the credit card after all, as a little sweetener. So, she was a shopaholic? What woman wasn't? He just needed to guide her in a more tasteful direction.

As his car moved off smoothly into the Rome traffic, a muscle pulsed in his jaw. He didn't mind the prospect of making over his fian-

cée; after all, style was something that had to
be learned. He knew because he'd done it. But
the image of her knocking back the champagne
stuck in his craw; the thought of her hostessing
a private dinner party filled with VIPs made his
skin go clammy with panic.

He thought then of the women he'd chosen as
lovers—their impeccable taste and style. Their
ability to seamlessly blend into any social en-
vironment without drawing adverse attention
to themselves, or him. Keelin was like a vivid
bird of paradise in comparison, and not in a
good way. It made him nervous. He was under
so much scrutiny because of his father that he'd
made it part of his life's ambition to never give
anyone an excuse to say, *Like father like son*.

He needed to project an air of unimpeach-
ability and stability, so people would trust him
professionally. His early life had been a litany of
violence, fear and ugliness. Gianni forced himself to take a deep breath. Keelin was not of that
world. She was just a bit garish. He could handle this, handle her. He would have to, because
marrying her meant a fast track to that respectability and acceptability he craved.

Gianni made a terse call to his assistants instructing them to make sure that a table had
been booked for dinner that evening. He sighed

and told himself that he was not dissuaded from his course just because his fiancée appeared all too coarse.

Keelin paced in the hotel suite, agitation making her movements jerky. She angrily kicked off the too-high shoes and opened another window to try and get rid of the noxious stench of perfume. As soon as Gianni had left she'd tipped the remaining contents of the glasses and bottle down the sink. She'd normally never touch the stuff, because it gave her thumping headaches and she could feel one brewing now.

She felt silly all over again, like a child playing dress-up, even though it was something she'd never indulged in because she'd been too busy adoringly trailing her father and looking for the smallest sliver of attention.

Also, she had not been prepared for the physicality of Gianni Delucca, or that he would have such an effect on her. It was disconcerting to say the least. She recalled the way his dark gaze had rested on her breasts and how a flash of heat had bloomed in her solar plexus. It had almost knocked her off her feet with its force.

She'd put blinkers on where men were concerned for a long time, after a traumatic incident in her last year of secondary level school.

She'd allowed herself to be vulnerable one time too many in a bid to seek the kind of male attention she'd been starved of from her father and it had resulted in a nightmare scenario that had shocked her out of her teenage angst and rebellion, and forced her to grow up overnight.

And until now no one had managed to make her feel remotely interested...but one look at Gianni and a slumbering part of her had woken right up.

She struggled to refocus and not think about her disturbing reaction to him—had she at least helped to convince him that she was a dizzy, overindulged, spoilt, shopaholic heiress with nothing between her ears except which celebrities might be staying in the hotel? The fact that she'd pulled that nugget of information from a headline she'd seen recently was a pure fluke.

She hoped it was doing the trick, and yet her act felt tawdry and flimsy now. She itched to get out of the too-tight dress and back into her favourite jeans and shirt, hair pulled messily into a knot on top of her head. She also longed to get out and see some of Rome's best known sights but unfortunately she couldn't play the part of herself right now. The stakes were too high.

For a long time Keelin had been weak enough to believe that a man's love and attention could fill the aching chasm in her soul, until she'd realised that it was only herself she could rely on for that sustenance, and that any such notions had been borne out of the lack of love her parents, and father in particular, had shown her. Freud would have analysed her in seconds, she'd been so pathetically transparent.

She'd come to understand that her focus had to be on concrete things like staking her claim on her family business—not wishy-washy notions that the unconditional love of a man would heal something that had broken a long time ago.

She assured herself she could do this. Gianni Delucca, and his disturbing brand of masculinity and fathomless dark eyes that had watched her far too carefully, was not going to deter her from her path.

That evening Gianni looked at his watch impatiently. Keelin was late, over half an hour late to be precise. For someone who was a stickler for punctuality, this grated on his still-jangling nerves. He'd never waited for a woman in his life. And he really did not relish overhearing the bar staff discussing rumours about a merger between the Harrington and the Chatsfield hotels. The last thing he wanted was a blaze of publicity to accompany this wedding. He was about to take out his mobile when he heard a hush descend on the exclusive Harrington Hotel bar and the hairs on the back of his neck prickled just before he looked up.

Keelin stood silhouetted in the doorway. Every head turned towards her. Gianni's eyes felt like they might explode out of his skull with a mixture of horror and unwelcome desire. He'd thought her dress earlier was short, but what she wore now would have made it look like a nun's habit. Her legs were completely bare, all the way up to where her modesty was just about preserved by the multicoloured lamé material of her dress. If it could even be called that.

A dress that skimmed out over womanly hips, dipping in to her small waist before curving sinuously over perfect breasts, tantalisingly visible in the open V that showed her flesh from neck to navel. The whole apparatus seemed to be precariously held in place by a gold hoop necklace that showed off her bare shoulders and arms.

That glorious red hair was bigger than it had been earlier, tousled and falling down behind her shoulders. Gianni was stunned. In shock. She looked like a call girl, but he felt the sharp kick of a lust so powerful it shocked him. Even as he was vowing that she would never, ever, appear in public with him again dressed like this.

And then that green, heavily made-up gaze settled on him and she raised an arm and called across the muted dimly lit bar, '*There* you are!'

Gianni winced and hated himself for it, as those long legs ate up the luxuriously carpeted distance and every head swivelled to follow her leonine progress. *Dio.* He'd seen more clothes on a Las Vegas showgirl. Even if she did move with an innately sensual grace that made his lust kick even more, confounding him. Was he really so rough underneath the respectable sheen he'd acquired that he appreciated this?

She reached him and stopped, her feet strapped into insanely delicate and ornate-looking gold high-heeled sandals. She obviously misread his interest and lifted one foot and said chummily as if he really cared, 'Just off the catwalk.' She rolled her eyes. 'Like, this is ridiculous. I could happily live and shop here for ever.'

Then she looked at him and clapped a hand to her mouth, eyes widening comically before she said, 'I can't believe I just said that! That's exactly what I'll be doing when we get married!'

Gianni was conscious of people looking and whispering and felt the prickle of that public scrutiny. And the need to get away from it. Which is what Keelin O'Connor *should* be helping him with, along with the kudos of joining forces with O'Connor Foods.

Angry that she was putting doubts in his mind again, Gianni took her elbow and said tightly,

'We should go, they're waiting for us in the restaurant.'

He gritted his jaw as a wave of that noxious perfume assaulted his nostrils again. Keelin was resisting ever so slightly and he looked at her. She made a small pout. 'Not even time for a weensy glass of prosecco?'

She gushed, 'I *love* prosecco, it's my new favourite drink. I had it in the spa this afternoon while I was getting my nails done.'

She shoved her hand under his nose then and waggled her fingers, showing off blood-red talons with a diamanté sparkle in the center of each one. His stomach lurched.

'You like?'

Gianni swallowed a sense of doom and took advantage of her momentary distraction to keep moving. 'They're fantastic.'

As they walked out of the bar and across the marbled lobby, Gianni noticed a few men almost get whiplash, their heads jerked so hard when they saw Keelin. To his disgust, he felt a very uncharacteristic urge to go and snarl at every one of those men to keep their gazes on their own women.

Keelin was chattering away, blissfully unaware, '…and I'm sorry I was late but I saw the most divine ruby necklace that would set off the peach resort dress I bought today, and then they had this thing on the Discovery channel about dogs—' She gripped his arm just as the maître d' of the restaurant caught his eye and ushered him in.

Gianni stopped and looked at her impatiently. 'Yes?'

She was gazing up at him, wide green eyes hopeful. 'Can we have a dog, please? I've always wanted a dog and Daddy never let me have one because he said I wasn't responsible enough.'

Her lower lip trembled. *Cristo*, was she about to cry? Gianni felt a clawing sense of claustrophobia, desperation. He dragged in a breath and reassured himself she was just excited and overwhelmed. It had been a mistake to give her the credit card; clearly she couldn't be trusted with unlimited funds. They'd talk over dinner and she wouldn't be as silly as he feared she was. She couldn't be.

'We'll discuss it, okay?'

Her green eyes shone with hope and gratitude, bright with unshed tears. 'Thank you, Gianni, so much. I know we're going to be really happy together. Daddy promised you'd take care of me, just like he has.'

Gianni didn't have time to let that last little bombshell land because the maître d' was leading them to the table. *Daddy promised you'd take care of me?* She was looking at him like a father figure? When he was looking at her and feeling a powerful mix of desire and disgust? Now he was freaked out on top of everything else.

An hour later, Gianni was also very much in doubt that any kind of happiness lay on the horizon. Irritation perhaps. Now that definitely featured. But he schooled his features and affected nothing but extreme interest in his fiancée, who he suspected could make an Olympic sport out of chattering inanely without drawing breath.

When she did pause to draw breath for one moment, Gianni took advantage and put up a hand to stop her next monologue about the way she felt reality-TV shows were *so true to life*.

'Keelin, we need to talk about this marriage.'

CHAPTER TWO

KEELIN WAS ACTUALLY relieved that Gianni had cut her off. She'd been ready to scream and had just been wondering what the hell she could witter on about next. But now she registered what he'd just said and suddenly air was in short supply. She forced a bright vacuous smile. 'Okay.'

He looked at her and she felt acutely self-conscious in the ridiculous outfit she was wearing. Her skin felt tight, sensitive. She was aware of her bare breasts brushing against the material of her dress or the material that called itself a dress. Her nipples were as hard as bullets and Keelin's frustration mounted.

'Look,' he said, 'I won't lie. I want this deal with your father and if that means marrying you, then I'm willing to do it, but I'm not such an ogre that I'll force someone into a marriage they don't want.'

The fact that he was actually being reasonable barely impacted. Keelin thought fast. If she fessed up now, then Gianni would walk away but tell her father that she'd called it off. And her father would never give her a chance to prove herself. It would be seen as one more rebellion, even though she'd stopped rebelling long ago.

No. She needed it to look like Gianni had rejected her, and at least that way she'd have proved her devotion to the company and her father would have to give her a chance.

Crossing everything she could, Keelin said breathily, 'My father loves me and I know he would only choose someone he really respected and trusted to marry me.' She widened her eyes. 'I only want what's best for O'Connor Foods and if I can help Daddy by doing this, then I'm happy.' She almost choked on the word *Daddy*.

Gianni's face was utterly expressionless and it made Keelin nervous. She couldn't read him. Was she overacting? Underacting?

He spoke slowly. 'You need to know this will only ever be a marriage born out of a business arrangement. This will never be about hearts and flowers, Keelin. Any children will be heirs to both our family legacies, keeping the names alive. That's why we're doing this. And if you think you can live with those circumstances, then I'll be happy to let your father know we'll marry in two weeks.'

Gianni's words resonated deep inside her.

This will never be about hearts and flowers.
The thought of falling in love with a ruthless businessman like Gianni made Keelin go cold all over. It would be the worst kind of repetition of a lesson she'd already learnt too well. It would never happen. She felt vulnerable just thinking about it and repressed a shudder.

She pushed that revelation down deep and giggled girlishly. 'After the way you've been looking after me already? I just know I'm going to love it here.'

A muscle in his jaw popped slightly at that and Keelin felt a rush of satisfaction. He couldn't be as sanguine as he looked. He would have a breaking point as to what kind of a wife he'd accept and she intended to find it.

Gianni put down his napkin. 'Very well then, I'll let your father know the good news.'

Keelin was already relishing the chance to get out of this man's disturbing orbit so she could think of her next move, but then he said, 'I have something for you.'

She looked at him, and then at the small velvet box he'd taken out of his jacket pocket. Damn. A ring.

Gianni opened the box and Keelin was almost dazzled by a huge square-cut diamond. It was a beautiful ring but not remotely original. Impersonal. Which was fitting. So why did something deep inside her feel ever so slightly disappointed at this evidence of Gianni's lack of consideration. She should be rejoicing!

'It's lovely.' She commented dutifully, and with what she hoped was a suitably dazzled smile.

'See if it fits.' Gianni plucked it out of the box and held it out.

Keelin slid the glittering ring onto her finger. It fit like a glove. As if the universe was conspiring with Gianni and her father to trap her. She dutifully moved her hand this way and that and thought to herself how far removed it was from the kind of ring she'd choose for herself.

Gianni was looking at his watch now and Keelin had a clear sense that she and the ring were on a checklist of things to do and she didn't like the old sensation of resentment that surged up like bile.

He looked back at her. 'It's been a long day. I'm sure you'd like to get some rest. I'll call the wedding planner in the morning to arrange a meeting.'

Keelin smiled sweetly and let Gianni guide her back out of the hotel restaurant even as she realised that she needed to up her game if she was going to really ruffle this man's incredible sense of complacency.

He turned to her at the lifts and smiled and for

a second Keelin forgot everything as she registered his sheer charisma and good looks. The lift doors opened and he held them back while she stepped in. His scent wound around her, making her feel a little hazy.

'*Buonanotte*, Keelin. Till tomorrow.'

She smiled when she wanted to grimace, hating his effect on her. 'Goodnight, Gianni.'

The lift doors closed on that far too distracting and darkly handsome face and Keelin sagged back against the mirrored wall. Delucca was about to learn that the meek and biddable wife he believed he'd acquired was anything but. And why did that suddenly feel like such an uphill battle?

For all of his apparent civility, Keelin had seen something hard in the depths of those dark eyes. Something immovable. And she wasn't sure if she wanted to tangle with it, no matter how determined she was.

It was the following evening before Keelin got to see Gianni again. He'd called her that morning and made his apologies but something had come up and he was going to be unavoidably detained in meetings all day.

Keelin had sweetly said not to worry about it. She was used to that treatment and couldn't let it get to her now. It wasn't as if she was actually going to have to deal with it after all.

In any case she had been busy all day, too, with the enthusiastic wedding planner and very obsequious Harrington Hotel PR manager. She'd almost felt sorry for them both, knowing that she was likely to make this wedding more *in*famous than famous.

Keelin checked her reflection in the mirror now and grimaced. She was wearing a glittery all-in-one black jumpsuit, complete with gold belt and slits up the side of each leg, visible when she walked. Together with vertiginous heels and copious amounts of gold jewellery, she was blingtastic.

When the knock came on her suite door she took a deep breath, not liking the flutters in her belly at the thought of seeing Gianni again. What was that about?

She opened the door and her hand tightened around the knob reflexively. He was even more devastating than she remembered. A dark shadow of stubble on his jaw. Shirt and tie, dark suit. A picture of casual Italian elegance yet with a masculine edge that was all too raw.

'*Buonasera*, Keelin, are you ready?'

Keelin nodded and noticed that his eyes dropped over her attire but he didn't compliment her. Because he couldn't bring himself to?

She hoped so, because she guessed with another kind of woman compliments would roll off his tongue. A rogue part of her shivered to think of standing before him in something far more *her*, and wanting his compliments. On the way down to the lobby he apologised again for being detained and she waved it aside, smiling. 'Please don't worry. I had a hectic day too.'

As he led her out of the hotel, she managed to keep up an inconsequential but hopefully very annoying chatter about all the minutiae of the wedding preparations, knowing how men in general detested anything like that.

She was still chattering while Gianni led her outside to a low-slung silver bullet of a sports car and then started again as soon as he sat into the driver's seat. Only the flicker of that muscle in his jaw told her she was hitting any kind of mark.

When she was drawing breath for another round of the most uninteresting conversation ever, Gianni interjected smoothly, 'I thought you might like to have dinner at my apartment? I have a view overlooking the Colosseum.'

Dammit. Those flutters were back at the prospect of being alone with this man. She made a small pout. 'I do love to people-watch but I suppose we have lots to discuss.'

He slid her a dark glance—and was that a hint

of irritation she could see around his mouth? She hoped so.

'Yes,' he agreed, 'we do have lots to talk about. I thought a quieter location might be more suitable.'

In any other instance Keelin would have appreciated his consideration but not now. But was she already going so far that he was reluctant to show her off in public? That had to be a good thing. It wasn't long before they were pulling up outside a formidable-looking building. Very old, but with an interesting architectural twist of lots of glass. Keelin liked it and found herself asking without thinking, 'Is this where you live?'

Gianni nodded as he parked the car with effortlessly sexy skill. 'It houses my offices too. I own the whole building.'

Keelin watched, a little dumbfounded by his admission, as he unfolded his tall powerful frame from the car and came around to her side to let her out. She had to put out a hand for his help and when his strong fingers closed around hers she felt the blood pulse between her legs.

No! Everything in her rejected this attraction.

He drew her up and they were so close they were almost touching. Keelin saw his eyes track down to the top of her jumpsuit and saw them flare. Panic gripped her. She was meant to be turning him off, not *on*. And that went for herself too.

Something resolute crossed his face as if he was fighting a similar battle in his own head. He stepped back and let her hand go. Keelin's blood was pumping so fast that she felt a little light-headed.

A doorman opened the door for them and Gianni introduced him as Lorenzo. Keelin smiled politely, and then they were ascending in the lift and the confined steel box was doing little to make her less aware of him. He seemed to take up a ridiculous amount of space.

When the doors slid open, there was a small plush corridor and Gianni was opening the door into the most stunning apartment Keelin had ever seen. She tried not to be impressed, to affect a blasé response, but it was a challenge not to let her jaw drop.

It was enormous, obviously the length and width of the building. Open plan but broken up by seriously luxurious discreet furnishings. Everything from the art on the walls to the rugs on the floors was perfectly pitched and placed. Seriously impressive.

She'd been facing away from Gianni and now he walked around in front of her. She quickly schooled her features into something more

disinterested and said, 'This is your only home
in Rome?'

Gianni nodded. 'What did you expect, *cara*?
A palatial villa on one of Rome's most exclusive hills overlooking gardens that belonged to
emperors?'

Keelin made a small shrug and said, 'I wasn't
sure what to expect.' Hoping to project disappointment.

Gianni said dryly, 'I do also own a villa in
Umbria.'

Keelin feigned delight. 'I believe it's beautiful there.'

'It is. I expect it's where you'll spend a lot of
time once we're married, but of course you'll
be welcome in the city whenever you need di-
version.'

Gianni walked over to a phone, saying, 'I'll
call the chef and let him know we're ready to
eat.'

It was just as well he was facing away from
her because Keelin was glaring at his back. He
expected that she'd be happy to be farmed out
to some crumbling Italian villa so that he could
get on with his own, obviously far more important, life?

Maybe he saw her out there with a brood of
dark-haired sons, grooming them to be the perfect heirs. For a second though, Keelin's anger

was pierced by something very scary to think of a miniature Gianni running around.

She crushed that image ruthlessly. This is exactly what her parents had done. Left her alone in their cavernous house for long months at a time. It was time to push Gianni off his complacent perch.

Within seconds of him making the call, discreet staff were preparing the dining room and he led her into the glass-walled space. Keelin did her best not to notice the stunning decor and assured herself she wouldn't be coming here for *diversions*.

Staff opened some champagne and she pushed down the queasiness, saying brightly, 'We should probably discuss the important stuff, like children.'

Gianni looked at her, cheeks flaring slightly with colour—because she was talking about this in front of his staff? He waited until they were alone and he lifted his glass of sparkling wine. 'You want to discuss that now?'

Keelin took a sip of the champagne and tried not to let her aversion to it show on her face. When she put her glass down she tried to look serious. 'Better now than never.'

She leant forward a little and said conspiratorially, 'Honestly? I didn't imagine even contemplating children until I'm in my thirties. But obviously in light of this engagement I've been thinking about it.'

She bit her lip as if this pained her to say. 'To be perfectly frank, the idea of labour and being pregnant is a serious downer. But I'd be open to adopting.'

She sat back again and elaborated as their starters were delivered. 'A friend of mine adopted a baby from Africa and she's so *cute*! All the big designers have kids' collections now, and naturally she has a nanny to take care of the day-to-day stuff.'

'You mean the child rearing.'

Keelin took a bite of food and pretended to be distracted. 'What? Oh, yes, that's what I mean.'

She risked a glance and Gianni was looking at her with a hard expression and Keelin feigned surprise and put her fork down. 'Oh, had you intended on having children, *for real*? Like, your own?'

His jaw was tight, he wasn't touching his food. 'Call me old-fashioned but yes, I had anticipated having children of my own.'

Keelin's anger flared again at the way he'd obviously decided he'd have no problem with children resulting from a cold and clinical union. She forced her irritation down and said pseudo-sympathetically, 'And you'd imagined your wife bringing them up in the villa?'

'Something like that. My mother was my main carer, not a nanny.'

Keelin rolled her eyes. 'Lucky you. I had a veritable parade of nannies.' She made a faint grimace. 'I wasn't the easiest child apparently, but I'm sure it's not hereditary.'

Gianni seemed prepared to let that little nugget go and frowned. 'Where was your mother?'

Keelin pushed down the old bitterness and said airily as if it hadn't mattered a jot, 'Oh, you know, with Daddy on trips, or away on holidays, or shopping. I was in boarding school most of the time.'

She looked at him after eating more of her starter and washing it down with champagne. 'You should probably hear it from me that I was expelled from four schools, including my last one, a finishing school in Switzerland.'

Gianni hadn't touched his starter and when the staff returned he let them take it. His eyes were hooded, dangerous. 'Hear it from you?'

Keelin shrugged. 'In case the papers pick up on it when they find out we're getting married.'

Gianni went rigid. He hadn't thought about that. 'You were expelled from all your schools?'

Keelin pouted. 'Well, not *all*. Not my primary one. Just the later ones, you know how teenage rebellion is.'

She continued chummily, 'But I can see how

good that discipline was for me so I'd be a big advocate of boarding school—the earlier, the better. There are lots of great schools in Ireland.'

Gianni fought down the urge to stand up and pace up and down. Keelin was *not* painting a good picture, and dammit, he hated feeling as if he was being made a fool of. Her father hadn't hinted at any of this. She was practically a delinquent! And yet she'd be only too happy to send any children they had down the same route! He'd always thought of boarding schools as upper-class nonsense.

Once again he forced himself to remain civil. 'May I ask what your transgressions were?'

Keelin ticked off her fingers. 'Being caught in a local bar, smoking, being caught with boys in the dorm, running away...'

Gianni felt disgust rise, not because they were serious crimes since they weren't especially, but he hated that evidence of someone from a life of privilege taking it so much for granted, exuding a kind of supercilious confidence that said she could do whatever she liked and get away with it.

And clearly she had the idea that her life would be going in the same direction as her mother's— that of leaving the care of her children to strangers or to a school. And they wouldn't even be *their* own children if she had her way! This conversation was also making a completely hitherto unexplored sense of protectiveness at the thought of a child of his own rise up within him.

It was too much. Gianni was feeling seriously claustrophobic. But then the main course arrived and he absently picked a suitable wine to go with the meat. Only to see Keelin wrinkle up her nose and say, 'I'll stick to the champagne, if that's okay. I can't abide wine.'

Gianni took a deep calming breath and tried not to dwell on that image of Keelin at important functions insisting on champagne when everyone else was drinking wine. He made a gesture to the chef's waiter and said urbanely, 'Of course, have what you like.'

Blissfully, for a moment as they ate, there was silence. And once Keelin wasn't talking and saying anything that was guaranteed to wind him up, he became uncomfortably aware of her.

In spite of the bling jewellery, big hair, lots of make-up and fake tan, she was clearly a beauty. Those eyes, especially when she widened them, threatened to distract him every time. And those lush lips. And the curves underneath the provocative silk of the jumpsuit, not to mention the flash of long shapely legs every time she moved. One thing was very clear—his body would marry this woman in a second, his head though was another matter.

When their plates had been cleared, Gianni's eyes narrowed on Keelin. For a moment she wasn't looking at him, or looking vacant, or chattering nonsensically, and he had the strangest notion that this was all some kind of elaborate—what? Was she deliberately sending him crazy? Making him doubt himself? Maybe he was being too hasty? Surely they could talk about these things, and if they had children, then perhaps she could be persuaded that a nanny was sufficient, and not necessarily a boarding school in the remote reaches of Ireland?

But just then she looked at him again, and a small frown marred her smooth forehead. 'There's something else I wanted to talk to you about.'

Gianni tried not to let his eyes drop to the voluptuous swell of her breasts. 'Yes?'

Keelin looked exceedingly uncomfortable; a faint blush stained her cheeks. 'I wanted to talk to you about sex.'

Gianni blanched a little. Had he been so obvious?

'You see,' she said hesitantly, 'the thing is that it's not for me.'

Gianni reacted on a deeply primal level. The

strength of the rejection he felt at that statement was surprising. 'Not for you?'

Keelin shook her head and looked pained. 'No. It's just—I hate it, to be honest.'

She shuddered delicately. 'All that fuss over nothing. All that sweatiness and bodily fluids. Ugh.'

She must have seen something on his face because she said with a kind of dawning comprehension, 'You didn't expect me to be innocent, did you? Because I've been with, like, tons of guys. Which is how I know I hate it.'

She just wouldn't want to be with him? The thought was like a red flag to a highly sexed male like Gianni. His jaw clenched. 'Of course I didn't expect you to be innocent.'

She continued in a conversational tone, 'I've thought about this a lot and while I'm not willing to have sex, I don't mind if you want to, you know, keep a mistress. You see,' she said hurriedly, 'that's really why I'd prefer to adopt.'

She sighed a big sigh of relief and smiled, as if she hadn't just landed a bomb between them. 'I'm glad I got that out there. I was worried.'

Then she put her hand on his and said, 'You're a good listener, Gianni. I'm so lucky to be marrying you.'

Her smile almost dazzled him. He was beginning to feel slightly ill. And then that anger surged again to think of her father giving him an impression of a mature, intelligent woman. He took his hand out from under hers, not liking how those cool fingers had felt on his skin.

He put down his napkin, finally tipping over the edge of his patience. 'I have no intention of taking a mistress during our marriage and I refuse to partake in the dubious exploitation of children and babies from third-world countries.'

He leant forward and tried to ignore those widening luminous green eyes. 'And as for sex? Maybe you don't like it because you haven't been doing it right?'

He had a sudden urge to take Keelin's face between his hands and stop that mouth from saying any more in the most effective way possible. His blood was pumping and he was afraid he might say something he'd regret, so he stood up abruptly. 'If you'll excuse me for a moment?'

Gianni barely waited for an answer; he strode out of the room, cursing the day Liam O'Connor had added the condition of a marriage of convenience to their contract.

He found himself pacing in his study, no less calm now that a few walls separated him and Keelin O'Connor. He could almost see her vacuous look of surprise.

Merda!

The woman was insufferable. The prospect

of marrying her was unconscionable. She didn't want children? And any children they did have or *adopt* she wanted to put in some stuffy boarding school? And she didn't like sex? Well, right now, he had no desire to prove her wrong no matter how rogue his physical reactions to her were. He cursed again.

He took his mobile out of his pocket and dialled. As soon as his friend answered he instructed him curtly to do some digging into Keelin O'Connor. Something he should have done from the very start, instead of taking her father's word that she would make him the perfect wife and partner as they went forward in business together.

He'd been so caught up with work and clearing his schedule for the merger and the wedding that he'd told himself he'd give Keelin the benefit of meeting her face to face to get to know her. He felt wrong-footed now.

He also had that persistent niggling sensation that something was amiss and he didn't like not knowing what it was. He wanted to go back into the dining room and tell Keelin that he'd made a mistake but even now something was stopping him. The prospect of letting the deal of a lifetime go. Wasn't there some way he could handle her? Women were usually the least of his worries!

But when Gianni did go back, something

made him stop in his tracks just where he could see through a crack in the doorway to the room beyond. Keelin was looking around surreptitiously before pouring the contents of her champagne glass into a nearby plant. He kept watching, feeling a rush of shock and anger along with something else—a kind of relief, as he saw Keelin check her watch and sigh heavily.

A mix of irritation, boredom and weariness crossed her face. Nothing close to the vaguely surprised expression when he'd walked out moments ago. She could be a different person.

Gianni was glad he'd just called his friend, because it was no longer a niggling suspicion that something was off about his fiancée's behaviour. It was a fact and he was determined to play her at her own game until he knew exactly what was going on.

About two hours later Gianni was standing back at the window of his study in his Rome apartment. He'd just seen Keelin back to her hotel, more distracted than he cared to admit by her wide pouting mouth and slightly tipsy demeanour. When he'd returned to the dining room she'd smiled brightly at him and for a second he'd almost wondered if he'd imagined what he'd seen through the crack in the door.

But then, when he'd put his hand over hers,

and promised that he would do his utmost to make their marriage work, he'd seen the panic flare in her eyes.

And now he burned with anger. No one took him by surprise. His life had been full enough of surprises and danger already. He'd carefully cultivated an existence that was as far removed from all that as possible.

But Keelin O'Connor had *almost* taken him in. A second conversation with his friend Davide just now had told him enough to know for sure that she'd been playing him.

For one thing, his supposedly vacuous fiancée had recently graduated from one of Dublin's most prestigious universities with the highest marks in her class, and a degree in business and economics. Not a degree in reality-TV trends, or the retail industry.

His mobile rang then and he answered curtly. His expression darkened as he bit out, *'Which club?'*

Gianni terminated the call and picked up the jacket he'd discarded earlier, his face grim. Anger turned to rage. Apparently his tipsy dizzy fiancée was not done with her sham act for the evening; she was now in one of Rome's most exclusive nightclubs making a spectacle of herself on the dance floor while paparazzi congregated outside, tipped off that Giancarlo Delucca's new fiancée was inside.

And tipped off by whom exactly? Gianni suspected he already knew exactly who and now he wanted to know *why* she was going to these lengths.

CHAPTER THREE

THE FLESHY SWEATY man grabbed Keelin around her waist and she put her hands on his to dislodge them, while trying to make it look like she wasn't really gritting her teeth. The idea of tipping off the paparazzi had seemed like a great idea about an hour ago after she'd sobered up with a few stiff coffees in her hotel room.

She'd had the strangest sensation after Gianni had returned to the dining room that he'd been looking at her with some kind of suspicion and it had been enough to galvanise her to pull out all the stops in her bid to deter him.

She forced another rictus grin at the dozen or so new best friends she'd made when she'd arrived at a VIP table and bought a round of champagne for everyone, courtesy of her fiancé's black credit card.

Just when she was about to recoil in disgust because the man's hot breath was getting closer and closer to her neck, his hands were removed and he was gone. To be replaced by someone infinitely taller, darker and more gorgeous.

Gianni. And just like that, her heart tripped.

She barely registered that he'd taken off his tie and his shirt was open at the top, giving him a rakish appeal. He came close and slid a hand around the back of her neck under her hair, tugging her shocked body towards him. He hadn't touched her intimately up to now. Keelin had to put her hands on his chest to steady herself and could feel nothing but steel-hard pecs.

Between her legs pulsed. She was so stunned to see him and be touching him that she could only look up into eyes so dark they were black.

'*Cara,*' he said, low and seductive, 'you really should have told me you wanted to go out after dinner. I would have taken you.'

'I—' Keelin stopped, her voice rusty. Not working properly. All of her usual inhibitions around men were dissolving away. Somehow he seemed to be able to reach right inside her, bypassing any rational consideration. Without even being aware of what she was doing her hands were spreading out over his chest as if to touch more of him. His smell was intoxicating, decadent and spicy. Very male.

She focused with effort. 'I didn't think you'd be into it.'

Gianni shook his head and smiled as if at

some private joke. '*Bella*, I'm into anything you're into. Now let's dance.'

He took Keelin's hand in an iron grip as he tugged her behind him to the dance floor. She felt sick, her legs wobbly in her high heels as she tried to assimilate this information and wonder how the hell Gianni had known where she was? Then she remembered tipping off the paparazzi and had her answer. No doubt Rome was full of people who would report back to him.

And without the fog of champagne clouding her judgement—she'd stuck to water since she'd arrived—she sensed an edgy tension coming from him. His hand on hers was hot and large. Experimentally she tried to pull away but his hold tightened. They got to the dance floor and the music worked against Keelin when it became slow and sexy, couples moving into sinuous embraces.

She was aware of people around them looking and whispering. This was not what she'd planned. At all. She'd planned on being all but carried out of the club, for maximum adverse news coverage.

But now Gianni was spreading his hands on her hips, and pulling her close, a wicked smile making his sensual mouth curve. But when she dragged her gaze up, there was something hard in his eyes. Keelin wobbled, and that suspicion returned. It was too huge to contemplate that he'd seen through her—so, weakly, she didn't.

She kept her hands firmly between them even though a very rogue part of her was seriously tempted to melt against him and twine them around his neck. Gianni moved a hand down to leave it resting uncomfortably close to the swell of her buttocks. Keelin's skin prickled into goosebumps of awareness.

He started to move in time to the music, their bodies fitting together far too well for Keelin's liking. Gianni's hand moved lower and Keelin's breath came quicker as he subtly pressed her hips into his even more. When she felt the hardness of his thick arousal against her belly her feet stopped and heat climbed up over her chest to her face. It was shocking. Shockingly *exciting*. And what was even more shocking was that her immediate reaction wasn't one of repulsion or fear.

Far too late Keelin tried to push him back a little. She was aware of how scantily dressed she was. The flimsy barrier of her silk jumpsuit affording no protection against his lean and aroused body.

She couldn't take her eyes off his. They were definitely hard now, and assessing. Panic flared. Keelin tried to put some space between them when all her body seemed to want to do was press even closer, imprint herself on him. Shocked at her reaction and angry now, remembering her agenda, she hissed, 'I told you, I'm not into *this* kind of thing.'

Gianni, not remotely fazed, queried with a raised brow, 'What? The *sex* thing?'

The music was low and throbbing, colluding with Keelin's heartbeat and body. She felt hot, flustered and out of her depth.

'Yes,' she hissed again.

Gianni's hands moved over her languorously, sensually, heightening every nerve ending in her body. He put his mouth near her ear and drawled, 'I think, *bella*, that we'll have to agree to disagree. You see, I think you will be very good at this *sex thing.*'

Keelin jerked her head back but it was too late. Just as she realised what Gianni intended and as he pressed her even closer, his head swooped and his mouth covered hers.

Keelin had been kissed before. Plenty of times. She'd become something of an expert in her teens, having perfected the art of kissing and going so far with boys without going further—until that traumatic night when she'd realised just how close she'd skirted to the edges of danger in a bid to seek male attention.

But Gianni was no lanky twenty-year-old testosterone-fuelled guy. He was all man. In his virile prime. And Keelin had no defences.

She was pressed so hard into his body that she could feel every taut sinew and hard muscle. His mouth on hers was firm, but demanding. Hard. His tongue touched the seam of her lips and without even being really conscious of what she was doing her mouth opened to him.

And then Gianni dominated her with sensual ease. His tongue swept in, stroking hers roughly, eliciting a response that made her legs weak, and hot sensations eddy between her legs. Her lower gut tightened with a kind of need she'd never felt before.

That finally sent some kind of awareness to her brain and Keelin pulled back from the kiss, eyes wide, staring into pools of dark brown.

Gianni's face was all stark lines and an unsmiling mouth. Keelin's lips tingled and felt swollen.

'I think it's time to leave, *cara*, don't you?'

He didn't wait for an answer; he just took his arms from around her and led her off the dance floor, taking her hand when people crushed around them. The music had changed to fast again and Keelin felt humiliated to imagine how they'd looked standing in the middle of energetically dancing couples while Gianni had demonstrated his easy dominance.

Everything in her chafed at that and when they got back up to the seating area she pulled her hand free. A girl was approaching with her short gold jacket and Gianni took it and held it out, for all the world the solicitous fiancé who was eager to get to a more private location.

Keelin had half a mind to stalk out and made a minute move but Gianni was blocking her way, as if reading her mind. She glared at him and he stared back.

With the utmost reluctance she put her arms in the jacket and let him settle it on her shoulders. Was it her imagination or was his slightly heavy-handed touch a warning?

When she turned again he had her clutch bag. She took it, just as he reached for her other hand again. But just like that kiss hadn't been a lover's kiss, his touch now was not gentle. It was an exercise in proving his strength and will.

And all she could think about was how she'd arched closer to him and let her tongue slip into his own mouth to explore all that heat and his intoxicating male taste. Humiliation burned her again; the minute he'd touched her she should have been flouncing off the dance floor, not pressing closer to him like a needy little kitten.

A sleek chauffeur-driven car was waiting outside the entrance to the nightclub. There was also a crowd of baying paparazzi. They started snapping as soon as Gianni appeared and he brought Keelin protectively forward with his arm around her, turning her into him so she was shielded.

The feel of all that taut musculature scrambled her brain cells again and he was saying something indistinct in Italian just before he all but pushed her into the back of the car and the door slammed. Before she had time to formulate a thought, Gianni was sliding in the other side and the car was pulling away.

Trapped.

Keelin was breathing hard. She looked at Gianni and there was ice in his expression. Her belly sank.

And then he said with more than a hint of steel, 'What the hell do you think you're up to?'

Gianni did not like to admit that he could still feel the imprint of Keelin's lush curves against his body from when he'd pulled her close on the dance floor. He'd meant it as an exercise in getting her away from that sweaty-handed creep, but all it had done was fire up his libido so much that he'd been sporting his first unwarranted erection in public since he was an oversexed teenager.

Dio. She should be turning him off with her over-the-top persona, but all he wanted to do was rip off that jumpsuit and get his hands on her naked curves. He could barely keep his gaze from roving over the firm swells of those generous breasts and those ridiculously long legs. He dragged his brain back from the edge.

'Well?'

She was all but curled into the door, looking at him as if he had two heads. And then she blinked, and straightened her shoulders. And pouted.

'I was having a good time, you know.'

Gianni curbed a grimace at her sulky tone. It was perfectly pitched and she could very well still be fooling him with it, if he didn't know better. A sense of humiliation made him smart again.

'Yes,' he said dryly. 'You looked like it with Federico Prezzi, one of Rome's most notorious porn kings.'

She couldn't disguise her instantaneous look of shock and disgust, but before she could manufacture some other false response Gianni put up a hand. 'Look, you might be happy to continue this ridiculous charade, but frankly, I've better things to be doing than hauling my fiancée out of nightclubs at three a.m.'

Her eyes went wide and wounded. 'Charade? I don't know what you're talking about.'

Gianni snorted. They were pulling up outside

the sleekly exclusive Harrington Hotel for the second time that night and he got out to open Keelin's door when being polite was the last thing on his mind. Especially when he saw a flash of one long bare leg through the slit in her jumpsuit as she got out.

He took her arm and all but marched her into the hotel. When they were in the lift she pulled free and looked at him accusingly. 'There's no need to manhandle me.'

Her big green eyes shone suspiciously and even though Gianni knew it was an act, he had to steel something inside of him, which only made his irritation levels rise further.

'I don't know why you're being such a grouch. I just wanted to have some fun. I *love* clubbing.'

I love clubbing. Something sparked in Gianni's brain. It was one of his pet hates. He could actually remember filling out one of those asinine *ten questions* for some weekend newspaper review magazine and that had been one of his answers. In fact, every single little thing about Keelin seemed to be perfectly pitched to annoy him or rub him up the wrong way.

The lift doors opened and, feeling very grim now, he took Keelin's arm again. He opened the door to her suite and let her go to precede him into the room. He hated to admit it but he knew that if he stayed and forced this conversation now, he might not be able to resist touching her because his anger and that feeling of having been made a fool of was pushing him to the limits of his control.

And that was enough to make him want to retreat. His father hadn't been able to control himself and Gianni had always had a very deep fear that he'd inherited his weakness. Not that he'd be violent, but that something of this rawness inside him might not be contained. He didn't want Keelin to see that part of him.

And he still didn't know enough. *Yet.*

She rounded on him with an injured expression on her face but before she could say anything Gianni folded his arms. *'Basta!' Enough.*

'I don't know what game you're playing, Keelin, but it's about as fake as the tan on that delectable body. I have an important meeting in the morning, early, so I'm not prepared to sit up all night and drag a confession out of you. When I see you tomorrow I expect to meet the *real* Keelin O'Connor.'

His gaze dropped down, taking in overtanned flesh and a blingy outfit more suited to Studio 54's heyday. 'And you can put that card I gave you to use and find some more suitable clothes to wear.'

Keelin's mouth opened, eyes wide, and Gianni cut her off. 'Save it for the morning, *cara. Buonanotte.*'

He turned at the door to see a decidedly mutinous look on her face now, eyes sparking with the intelligence he'd caught a glimpse of in his apartment. Unexpectedly he felt a flare of excitement to recognise that a part of him relished getting to know *this* woman.

'And don't even think of trying to pull any more cute stunts. You make one move out of this hotel room and I'll know about it in seconds.'

She sputtered indignantly, 'You can't do—'

But he'd closed the door.

Keelin was left looking at a blank space. For a long moment she stood in shock and then the pain of her feet in the heels impinged and she kicked them off angrily. *He knew.* He had somehow figured it out.

A sense of panic warred with relief that she didn't have to put on this elaborate act any more. And also trepidation, to know that she'd have to face that man as herself. She went into the bathroom, looked at her reflection in the artfully lit mirror over the enormous sink. Her eyes were wide and bright. Cheeks flushed. Her gaze dropped and she sucked in a breath to see the stark outline of her nipples pressing against the flimsy silk of her jumpsuit.

She could recall all too easily how she'd wanted to rub them against Gianni's chest in the club, to assuage the burning ache. *Dammit.* Once again she felt that vulnerability to know that he had a unique effect on her, cutting right through her defences. She wasn't prepared for this unprecedented physical reaction to him. It was as if when he touched her something fused in her brain.

She was afraid of Gianni's effect on her, that if he kissed her again she wouldn't be able to protect herself in time. And that he might make her feel as powerless as she had when—

She closed her eyes against the memories and sucked in a deep breath.

This was why she'd avoided any kind of intimacy before now, in spite of the picture she'd painted to Gianni. She assured herself resolutely that he wouldn't be kissing her again because she'd do whatever it took to persuade him that this union was wrong.

When Keelin woke the following morning after a fitful sleep, she felt a wave of optimism—perhaps she was wrong and Gianni just suspected something? Galvanised by the thought that all was not lost, she dressed again with inappropriate zeal in a figure-hugging red dress, and made her way to the entrance of the hotel, determined to go shopping again as if nothing had happened and hope for the best.

But when she got to the door, a tall dark familiar figure was waiting for her. She cursed silently as he approached her and took her arm before bending and pressing a kiss to her cheek. Her heart spasmed.

He pulled back and she looked at him. He smiled but his eyes were hard. '*Buongiorno, cara.* So nice of you to come down and meet me.'

'But I wasn't, I was—'

But Gianni wasn't listening. He was all but frog-marching her out of the hotel to where his sleek chauffeur-driven car was waiting. She was in the back of the car and he was on the other side in a louche sprawl before she could get her breath and register that they were moving away from the hotel.

Keelin had given in to the bitter tang of defeat. He knew.

'Where are we going?' she asked, feeling mutinous.

'My apartment. We need to talk.'

Keelin looked out of her window, refusing to so much as glance in his direction for the duration of the journey, furiously trying to think of what he might say. And how much did he know? The fact that he might know of her degree made her feel inordinately exposed. Old and familiar urges rose. To rebel. To run. But she couldn't. She had to be smart and roll with the punches and ensure that no matter what happened she'd come out on top and her father would be forced to acknowledge her role in their family's company. Solo. Not married.

A memory of when she'd been about eleven years old sprang into her head. She'd been with her paternal grandfather in one of the O'Connor Foods factories. It had been a very rare visit—usually she was never taken to the factories. Huge articulated lorries had been peeling away, out of the forecourt, on their way across Europe with foods, and her father was standing in the middle, like the conductor of an orchestra.

She'd been mesmerised by all this industry and the family legend that it had all originated from one field and a herd of cattle in the west of Ireland.

In her mind at that moment she'd made the connection between her father's obsession with work and his lack of obsession with *her*. She'd turned to her grandfather and said excitedly, 'When I grow up I want to work with Daddy.'

Her grandfather had looked at her with disappointment lining his old face and had bent down to her level and said very clearly, 'That won't ever happen, Keelin. If you had a brother, maybe—'

Even now, she could remember the awful hollowing-out sensation, and the feeling of guilt, that she wasn't enough, because she was a girl. She'd looked out over the forecourt again and had realised that, because of her, all of this would cease to exist some day. And that's when she'd vowed to do everything she could to show her father that she could be enough.

'We're here.'

Keelin blinked and looked to see the by-now-familiar building. A sense of déjà vu assailed her as Gianni got out and came around to let her out. She felt silly, trussed up like some kind of over-the-top reality-TV star.

She pettily refused to take his hand of help and got out herself, less elegantly than she would have liked. He just shrugged minutely and led the way into his building.

The elevator felt even more claustrophobic this time, because now she knew what it felt like to be in Gianni's arms, his mouth on hers. That hard body pressing against hers. Her face was flaming by the time the lift came to a stop and she almost fell out in her haste to put some space between them.

It was almost a relief to step into his palatial

apartment again and she quickly moved over to one of the windows, dreading what was coming.

Reluctantly she turned to look at Gianni and he was stern and formidable. Distant. Perhaps she could convince him to see sense? A small voice somewhere laughed at that. Facing up to the unpalatable suspicion that he would not rest until he knew everything, Keelin steeled herself and said bluntly, 'I don't want to marry you.'

His expression didn't change but she saw a flash of something in those dark eyes. 'Did it occur to you to say this when we met first and I gave you the opportunity instead of putting on the elaborate act?'

She flushed as his gaze narrowed on her. He came closer and Keelin could sense the tension reaching out to touch her like the sharp end of a nail across her skin. This was a man who didn't appreciate being messed with. And she'd been like a mouse teasing a lion for the past two days.

She lifted her chin and avoided answering that question directly. 'I'm sorry if you've been inconvenienced, but I have no intention of marrying you.'

Gianni was grim. 'And would you care to explain why you didn't walk away when your father proposed this arrangement?'

Not really. Keelin swallowed and crossed her arms defensively. There was no way she could physically move past Gianni. He seemed to take up all the space in the room. *Hell.* Eventually, with the utmost reluctance, she said, 'If I walk away, then my father will effectively disown me.'

The prickle of exposure to have said that out loud made her irritated now. She didn't want to feel any vulnerability here in front of this man.

Gianni mirrored her, folding his arms across his chest, making the muscles of his arms stand out against the cloth of his suit.

'Need I point out that by marrying me you'll become obscenely wealthy?'

Keelin flushed, angry to be so aware of him. 'It's not about the money.'

He arched a brow. 'Could have fooled me. You spent a small fortune yesterday.'

She felt slightly sick to think of it now. 'That was just part of...' She faltered and stopped. 'I can send the clothes back.'

His voice was cooler than the Arctic. 'Don't worry, my assistants are already in the process of doing that. So this was your grand plan? To try and convince me that you were entirely un-suitable?'

Some of Keelin's anger drained away. 'In a nutshell, *yes.*' She felt supremely foolish now to have underestimated Gianni so much.

He snorted derisively. 'You thought that if you

could make me believe you were the total opposite of what I wanted, then I'd show you the door?'

Keelin looked at him, determined not to let him intimidate her. 'You have to admit it, you had doubts.'

As if Gianni Delucca would admit such a thing. And then he took the wind out of her sails, saying, 'You're not the only one who did some digging.'

Keelin's stomach dropped. She'd been afraid of this but tried to brazen it out, unconsciously tossing her hair over her shoulder. 'And?'

His gaze became speculative. 'Surprisingly enough in spite of your teenage fits of rebellion no photographic evidence showed up of you behaving as the vacuous socialite you'd have me believe you are.

'What *did* turn up,' he continued, 'was evidence of a model student in college, recently graduating with flying colours.'

Once again the memory stung of all her friends celebrating with their adoring families while she'd had no one there for her. The momentary self-pity mocked her and added a bitter twinge to her voice. 'Don't let that fool you, Gianni, it served a purpose. If I'm to take over my family business some day I'm not so arrogant as to assume I don't need any preparation.'

Another derisive-sounding snort. '*You* take over O'Connor's? A global company?'

Keelin saw red. 'Just because I'm a woman—'

Gianni cut her off with ice-cold precision. 'It has nothing to do with you being a woman. Some of the best CEOs in the world are women. It has to do with the fact that you have zero experience and seem to think it should be handed to you on a platter.'

The unfairness of Gianni's attack made something hot prickle behind Keelin's eyelids. Aghast that he might see how high her emotions were and afraid of what might come out of her mouth, she whirled around and went to stand at a nearby window, arms even tighter across her chest. She felt intimidated and cornered. *Misunderstood.*

When she was more in control she turned around again and it was as if she was seeing Gianni for the first time. His sheer dark good looks and charisma reached out almost like a taunt.

'You don't get it, Delucca. My father believes that because I'm a woman I'm not entitled to inherit my place in the family business. All I've ever wanted is a chance to prove to him that I'm capable of being his heir. That's the only reason I agreed to this farcical arrangement, because he literally gave me no other choice. But I have no intention of going through with it, and *you* are going to be the one to call it off, or so help me I'll attract all the attention you don't want in a convenient wife.'

Danger crackled in the air between them but Keelin fought not to back down.

Gianni sneered faintly. 'You expect me to walk away from the deal of a lifetime because you're too scared to stand up to Daddy Dearest?'

Keelin gritted out, 'He's not my Daddy Dearest, far from it.'

She realised she was breathing heavily and that her blood was high. Damn this man for pushing her buttons and making her blurt everything out.

Gianni's narrowed gaze was far too assessing, and then he said silkily, 'Perhaps you should have this discussion with your father when you see him this evening?'

Keelin felt her blood go cold. 'My father? What are you talking about?'

Tension stretched between them, as brittle as glass.

'I've arranged an engagement party for this evening in The Harrington's penthouse suite. It'll be an intimate exclusive party to introduce you to my friends and business associates.'

Keelin's heart thumped hard. Once. Her mouth felt dry. 'Since when?'

Gianni looked all too innocent and yet as sinful as the devil. 'Oh, I'm sorry, *bella*, did I not mention it before now?'

'No,' she responded tightly as dread skittered over her skin that he was turning the tables on her, and at the thought of this being made public. Official. 'You didn't.'

Gianni smiled and it was the smile of a shark. 'Please forgive me. It must have escaped my attention. Your beauty continues to—how do you say in English?—divert me...'

The compliment rang hollow with insincerity, and she was nothing like his usual women. He spoke English better than she did. But it was effective enough to bring back the memory of the throbbing beat of the music in the club and the feel of Gianni's tongue sliding into her mouth with carnal intent, the way his body had felt against hers.

She blurted out, 'Why are you doing this?'

Gianni ignored her question and since when had he moved closer? Now only a couple of feet separated them, his arms down by his sides. Keelin felt hot.

'Both your parents will be there. Our guests of honour. They fly in this evening. They're staying at The Harrington. Your mother said something about wanting to see the plans for the ceremony and the reception.'

Keelin's brain froze. She looked into those

fathomless dark eyes that were utterly guileless and yet not. Vulnerability hit her right between the eyes at the thought of her parents suddenly showing a level of support and interest that had never existed until now. And at the thought that Gianni was colluding with them, which of course he was. So why was she feeling a bizarre dart of hurt?

'How dare you do this without consulting me?'

Colour slashed Gianni's cheeks and Keelin felt something else vibrate in the air between them, something much more physical.

'I dare because you were hell-bent on making me a laughing stock and that is not going to happen.'

Frustration mounted inside Keelin to have him so baldly lay out how helpless she was. And then she became blisteringly angry at him for accepting this status quo just because he was greedy for success and more power.

She lashed out. 'Did you seriously not question why a complete stranger would agree to marry you? Are you so arrogant? So full of your own importance that it didn't even seem strange?'

Not waiting for an answer, she went on. 'I mean, who in their right mind would agree to marry a man who has links to the Mafia?'

Gianni went very still, not that he'd been moving around much before, but Keelin had felt his restless energy. And now it was as if he had sensed his prey and every muscle was locked tight in preparation to pounce. His hands were out of his pockets and by his sides, hands curled to fists.

Shivers raced over Keelin's skin. She'd pushed a button. A big one. And it didn't make her feel a sense of triumph.

He was cold. 'I do not have links to the Mafia.'

Keelin pushed down a sense of having stepped over a huge mark. 'But your father—'

He cut her off brutally. 'My father is dead, and you will not mention this again. Damn you.'

Keelin had only the merest sliver of warning before Gianni's arms reached out to grab her upper arms and he hauled her into his chest, his mouth covering hers with such precision that she wondered if somehow he'd read her mind and known that she'd been thinking about that kiss endlessly since last night.

And just as she'd feared, being kissed by him again was setting off a chain reaction of tumbling all of her defences like dominoes, making her pliant, making between her legs throb and ache. Her hands were caught between them and from somewhere that hadn't yet been enslaved by his touch she curled her hands to fists and pushed, wrenching her head back.

She opened her eyes and saw nothing but black. She pushed herself free, out of his hands, and stepped back shakily. 'I don't want this, I don't want *you*.'

Gianni's mouth twisted. 'You might not want this situation but you want *me*, as much as I want you.'

And then before she could respond, he said, 'Are you a chess player, Keelin?'

It was clearly a rhetorical question when he continued, 'I'm not willing to call this wedding and merger off, not in a million years. And you can't walk away because you'll be left out in the cold—so it would appear that we have a stalemate.'

The air seemed to throb and shimmer between them with heat and tension, and Gianni stared at her for such a long moment that Keelin almost begged him to stop, but then he lifted his hand and looked at the watch on his wrist. He looked at her again, coolness in his eyes now. 'A stylist and hair and make-up team are on their way here to get you ready for the party. They told me it would take that long to get rid of the day-glo look. I'll be back later to pick you up.'

Clearly nothing she'd said had made one dent in his bid to secure this deal with her father.

He was steamrollering ahead and taking her with him.

She put her hands on her hips, aware of the little betraying tremor. 'Now wait just a minute, if you think that I'm going to—'

The words died in her throat when Gianni stalked closer, a look of dangerous intent on his face. Perversely it didn't scare Keelin that he might kiss her again; it excited her. But he didn't.

'This marriage is happening, Keelin. Now more than ever. And if you don't start washing off that persona you've been playing with for the past forty-eight hours, then I'll be more than happy to take you to the shower to help you. So what's it to be?'

CHAPTER FOUR

THAT EVENING GIANNI was still struggling to control his temper. When Keelin had mentioned his *father* and *Mafia* he'd seen red. For some reason the fact that she'd levelled that accusation at him had stung more than most. Enough to want to silence her by putting his mouth over hers and losing himself in the inferno of need that had spiralled up through his body, almost taking his head off.

Cristo. No woman had ever made him so hot, or hot-headed, in his life. Up until now he'd chosen women he desired but none of them had made him feel out of control enough to want to devour them, or had reduced him almost to some kind of animalistic state. And that made him very nervous. He'd considered his father an animal whenever he'd come home drunk and taken out his aggression on his wife. Or when he'd disappeared for days on end only to reappear with money and blood-spattered clothes.

His father's poisonous legacy was something Gianni desperately wanted to dissociate himself from. It symbolised everything that was dark and violent and base. And that was not him. Yet, he took one look at Keelin and felt nothing but feral desire. Disconcerting as it was, he was sure that once he'd slaked his desire, her hold on him would decrease.

He'd changed in the dressing room attached to his office and the classic tuxedo he wore now made him feel constricted when it never had before. He could remember his first occasion wearing a tuxedo to a glittery event and how for the first time in his life he'd received looks of admiration, respect.

As constricting as the suit might feel right now, *this* was what separated him from his father's legacy—this ability to appreciate the fine things in life and to know that the way forward was through promoting integrity and honesty. Building a business to be proud of. The business his grandfather had set up, before his own son had taken it and crushed it to the ground.

Earlier, when Gianni's assistant had shown stylists with clothes rails and an assortment of other suitably qualified people up to his apartment, he'd found himself almost relishing the thought of Keelin's expression when she knew she had no choice but to comply.

But then his conscience smarted when he thought of what she'd revealed about her reasons for wanting out of this marriage. He'd scoffed at her intentions to be a part of her family's business, yet didn't she have that right? After all, at least he'd had the shell of his grandfather's business to build an empire upon and after a lot of blood and sweat and ingenuity he was finally here, or would be, once he merged with O'Connor.

He had to admit that Keelin's evident determination to succeed no matter what inspired a grudging sense of kinship within him. But he couldn't let the niggle of his conscience sway him. He needed this deal. Now more than ever.

His chief executive advisor had just informed him that the very rumour that Delucca Emporium was merging with O'Connor Foods had caused a soar in stocks. The news wouldn't be officially announced until the day after the wedding took place—as per O'Connor's request, even though they'd already signed contracts.

So he couldn't afford to let this momentum drop now. He needed every ounce of positive press to convince people he could be trusted, and as much as he might sympathise with Keelin's bid for independence, she was not going to stand in his way. He'd worked too hard for this chance.

Keelin hated that she felt bizarrely excited. She *should* be steamingly angry. The threat of Gianni washing the spray tan off her body himself had been enough to galvanise her into the bathroom earlier that day, locking herself inside and scowling when she heard his mocking, 'Later, *cara*,' through the door.

A veritable army had then appeared in the apartment when she'd emerged from the shower with skin pink from scrubbing and had proceeded to take her in hand, undoing all of the hard work she'd put in to appear as trashy as possible.

And now she hated to admit that she didn't look a million miles off what she'd choose to look like, if she didn't have a war of personal independence on her hands.

She was wearing a strapless dark green dress that made her eyes stand out. Fitted around her breasts, it fell in soft swirls of silk and chiffon from below her bust to the floor where she wore delicate high-heeled sandals.

She was back to her habitual paleness, and felt a little naked now without the copious amounts of make-up and tan. Her hair had been teased and coiffed out of its natural wildness and lay over one shoulder in glossy soft waves, held back on the other side by a long diamond comb.

Make-up was subtle and enhanced her features. Her cheekbones stood out, and her mouth looked even bigger than usual. She wanted to scowl at the reflection in the bathroom mirror as she inspected herself, but in truth she felt a funny catch in her throat at the thought of Gianni seeing her like this, as if she was meeting him for the first time all over again.

'Keelin?'

Speak of the devil. Her heart thumped hard and she took a deep breath, cursing the fact that she'd allowed herself to get distracted enough not to analyse what had been said earlier and figure out what her next step would be.

She heard Gianni come closer. 'Keelin, so help me, if you're not here and ready—'

He appeared in the doorway of the master bedroom en suite and stopped talking, those dark eyes raking her from head to toe. Heat climbed up over Keelin's chest to her neck and face.

She registered how gorgeous he was in his tuxedo, clean jaw, hair short. Suddenly there was no air; her skin felt tight and hot. Terrified he might see her reaction she moved forward and pushed past him. 'I am here.'

When she was on the other side of him the

hardness of his body registered on her brain with a searing flash of heat. She stalked out into the main living area, desperate to put some space between them, sucking in a deep breath. When she turned around again, Gianni had followed her and was leaning against the door frame, hands in pockets, eyes hooded and unreadable.

Keelin's hands clutched the bag that went with the dress. She wanted to squirm; no man had ever looked at her so intently.

'Well, well, well,' he drawled softly. 'I knew there was a gem hiding underneath all that artifice.'

Keelin was about to say something waspish but Gianni added, 'But I had no idea how beautiful that gem would be.'

For a moment she felt stunned. Even though he'd kissed her, somehow this felt more intimate, as if he was stroking his tongue along hers all over again, that hard mouth demanding she give up her softness to him. Demanding she expose all her weaknesses and vulnerabilities.

At a loss as to how to respond, and feeling gauche when she recalled how she'd noticed he hadn't complimented her the previous evening, Keelin just said, 'Save your breath for the woman who'll become your fiancée for real some day. She'll be far more appreciative.'

Gianni stood away from the door and came towards her. Keelin's feet were glued to the floor. He stopped far too close and answered, '*Cara*, you're the only fiancée I'm ever going to have, so you might as well give in to the inevitable—unless you're willing to walk out that door right now, we will be getting married in two weeks.'

The fact that Keelin couldn't seem to find the urge to walk away from Gianni now that she had the opportunity was not as annoying as the suspicion that it had less to do with her father's ultimatum and intransigence and more to do with the fact that something enigmatic in his black gaze held her to the spot.

An hour later Keelin's feet burned in her high heels. She was in a sleek and sophisticated private suite at the Harrington Hotel surrounded by beautiful and equally sleek people with white besuited waiters moving through the crowd carrying trays of sparkling champagne, and yet all she could see were the women openly lusting after Gianni, and sending her less than friendly glances. She felt like saying to them, *Take him!* while alternately battling a very curious urge to gouge their eyes out.

He bent close and said by her ear in his deep voice, 'Your parents are here.' Instantly she tensed all over, an inevitable reaction, her hand tightening on her glass of champagne. The drink she'd not even touched. No point in pretending she liked it any more.

She barely noticed Gianni sending her an assessing sidelong glance as her mother came forward with arms outstretched to envelop Keelin in a stiff hug and a noxious wave of perfume. Keelin couldn't help tensing even more. She'd learnt long ago that these rare displays of affection were for appearances only, never to be repeated in private.

Her father gave her a kiss on the cheek. Equally awkward. Keelin felt old emotions rise—a mix of anger, disappointment and frustration, and swallowed it down with effort.

Her mother was oblivious, beaming at Gianni and gushing, '*So* pleased to meet you, Mr Delucca. Liam's told me all about you. You'll take care of our beloved Keelin, now won't you?'

He was oozing charm as they shook hands. 'Call me Gianni, please.'

Beloved Keelin. It had been the wrong moment to take a reflexive sip of her drink; it promptly went down the wrong way and Keelin had a coughing fit, earning a familiar look of irritation from her mother and a hand on her bare upper back from Gianni which was far more disturbing. Keelin wasn't someone who felt comfortable around tactile people but whenever Gianni touched her she felt the disturbing urge to close her eyes and purr gently.

'Okay, *cara*?'

His careless endearment sent shivers through her. She nodded and blinked quickly and croaked, 'Fine.'

His fingers spread out now, just above the bodice of the dress, and his touch became more caressing. The kind of touch anyone might expect of a man to his fiancée.

But there was something else in it too; as she stood there by Gianni's side and faced her parents she had the bizarre sense for the first time in her life of not standing alone against them. Which was crazy because Gianni only wanted this marriage as a business deal; he wasn't genuinely interested in the kind of support that should come with a *real* marriage.

That galvanised her to move subtly away from his touch and she hated how she felt bereft when his hand dropped. She sent him a dark look for having this effect on her but he merely raised a brow in return. Completely bemused.

An arm went through hers. 'Darling, let's let the men talk boring work and tell me all about your plans for the wedding.'

Keelin blinked at her mother before letting herself be led away, fuming inwardly at the implication that she couldn't be part of that conversation. And as if for all the world this was a genuine wedding and she and Gianni were some sort of besotted couple. She said acerbically, 'Don't you mean discuss the plans for this business arrangement?'

Her mother darted a glance around and then pulled Keelin into a secluded corner. Gone was any attempt to feign affection and the truth was visible of an attractive woman who was ageing and not happy about the process or the fact that her daughter was far more beautiful than she'd ever been.

'What is wrong with you? That man is young, handsome and rich. You could do a lot worse, you know.' Her mother sounded almost peevish.

Keelin sighed inwardly. That was all her mother understood—the currency of a rich husband and being socially acceptable. After all, she'd made it her life's work, especially when she hadn't been able to have more children after Keelin, which she'd borne a totally irrational sense of guilt about for as long as she could remember.

Keelin valiantly pushed aside old wounds. 'You mean worse than have a chance to work for the family business and be independent?'

Her mother all but snorted. 'Darling, I've never understood this obsession you have, and why work when you don't have to?'

Her darker green eyes narrowed on her daughter. 'I really hope you're not going to be difficult about this. Your father will be very angry—'

Keelin cut her off crisply. 'Don't worry, I've already been told what'll happen if I walk away.'

Dolores O'Connor didn't even have the grace to look remotely concerned or guilty. 'Most girls would give their eye teeth to be in your position.'

Keelin felt a prickling sensation on the back of her neck just before an arm slid around her waist and a large *hot* body came alongside hers. Once again she had to battle that urge to just *sink* against him. She stiffened against the tide of sensations that washed through her. It only showed up a lingering pathetic need for some kind of male approval.

Her mother gave a completely *un*subtle look to Keelin and excused herself with a wholly inappropriate girlish giggle. Keelin rounded on Gianni when they were alone, dislodging his arm from around her.

'What's with the PDA? I don't think anyone could care less how authentic we are.'

She glanced around at the chattering crowd and surmised, 'It's not as if all these people are actually in love with their partners.'

Gianni tutted and drawled, 'So cynical and so young. What made you like this, Keelin?'

She looked at him. 'And you're not?' The man

oozed cynicism. She hated that he could slide a blade under her skin so neatly and declared, 'I need a drink.'

He looked pointedly at her champagne and she answered expressively, 'Of something I actually like.'

She went to move around him and he stopped her with a hand on her upper arm again, fingers brushing far too close to the swell of her breasts.

'No one else might care how authentic we are, Keelin, but I do. Do I need to remind you how authentic we can be if I touch you? So when we're in public we are *together*.'

Keelin fought down the panic at the thought of Gianni demonstrating how weak she was in front of all these people and said as witheringly as she could, 'I wouldn't have had you down as a romantic fantasist, Gianni.'

Childishly pleased that she'd had the parting shot, she pulled her arm free and walked away, steering well clear of where her parents were talking to another couple nearby. The last thing she needed now was for her father to join in loading on the pressure.

By the time Keelin got to the discreet bar in the corner of the room and ordered a drink, she was wondering what was stopping her from just walking out the door and to hell with the lot of them.

She turned around and surveyed the room. Some of the world's most powerful and important people were here. People whose opinions counted and mattered. And that's why she couldn't walk away. Not yet. Because she wanted this too—to be counted and listened to. Given a chance. And also, disturbingly, Gianni's darkly handsome face kept flashing into her mind.

As if loath to let her have that parting shot, he approached her through the crowd now, eyes on her in such an assessing way that her skin rose up in goosebumps of anticipation.

He stopped before her and looked at the bottle of beer in her hand. 'Must you?'

She gritted her jaw and vowed that she would get through this experience and come out on the other side with everything she'd ever wanted. And for it to make not walking away worth it.

In answer, she took a healthy swig from the bottle and dared him to take it off her and replace it with something far more genteel and ladylike.

Gianni swallowed down the urge to rip the bottle out of Keelin's hands. But if drinking out of a beer bottle was going to be the worst of her behaviour tonight, then he'd put up with it.

She stood out with her pale skin and red hair like a bird of paradise against a much duller background. And it galled him that he'd observed her smiling at people all evening, only for that smile to fade as soon as he came close.

It wasn't a smile as wide as the one he'd seen in the photo at her father's office but it was close. And since when had that become some kind of barometer? He cursed himself now as he steered Keelin back towards the crowd to introduce her to some colleagues. And he also pushed down the niggle of curiosity about how she'd been with her parents. She'd almost recoiled when he'd mentioned that they'd arrived and it certainly hadn't been a happy family reunion.

God knew, he had the experience of despising his father until the day he'd died, so he knew antipathy when he saw it. But in spite of that relationship, he and his mother were close, even if she did insist on living outside of Rome in the family home, keeping the house like some kind of mausoleum to his father's memory. Gianni had never been able to understand his mother's slavish devotion to the man who had made her life miserable on a regular basis. He'd decided long ago that if that was love, then he could quite happily live without it.

Thinking of that now made Gianni feel a little raw. He knew he didn't want love so why was he even remembering that? But right then he also didn't want a wife who was hell-bent on thwart-

ing him at every turn. Acting on impulse, count-
ing on Keelin's ambition, he pulled her aside just
before they entered the throng again and said in
a low voice, 'If you do want out, Keelin, truly,
then this is your chance.'

Caught by surprise Keelin looked at Gianni and
saw the gleam of challenge in his eyes just before
he deftly caught a passing waiter and swapped
her bottle of beer for a glass of champagne. Then
he took up a small spoon from a nearby table and
tapped his glass so that a melodic ring chimed
out and everyone stopped talking and turned to
face them.

Keelin's stomach went into freefall. What the
hell was he up to?

When they had everyone's attention, and
Keelin could see her parents looking at them
with faux fondness, Gianni said in a voice that
commanded attention, 'Thank you all for coming this evening to help celebrate my engagement to this beautiful woman.'

Keelin's sense of nausea rose. Gianni pulled
her close and raised his glass. 'To my fiancée,
Keelin, with whom I look forward to a very successful, *long* and enduring partnership.'

Everyone clinked glasses and saluted them,
taking drinks of the sparkling wine. When
they'd done the toast Gianni let her go slightly

and looked down. Keelin met his gaze with a murderous one of her own. As every second passed she felt as if she were being hurtled further and further away from where she wanted to be.

But he wasn't finished. He added now, 'If you could indulge us a few moments more, I do believe my fiancée has something she wishes to say.'

Comprehension sank in. He was daring her to do her worst. To declare in front of everyone that this was a sham, or worse? Walk out the door? She recognised that this was a moment of no return. Everything would be dictated by what she did now. Gianni was calling her bluff, asking her to prove how badly she wanted out of this arrangement.

All she had to do was to say the words and walk away. She could already imagine the look on her parents' faces. Her father's going red, her mother's shock and embarrassment in front of all these important people.

And for a moment she was sorely tempted. She opened her mouth. And then she caught Gianni's eye; he was taunting her for his amusement. And that was the thing that firmed her resolve. She would not let him goad her into jeopardising everything.

So she channelled her anger and frustration to be so caught and smiled brightly. 'I'm a woman who believes that actions speak louder than words.'

And then she deliberately put her drink down on a nearby table and turned to her fiancé. She put both hands around his face and caught his look of shock a second before their mouths met. She poured all of that anger and frustration into a bruising-hard kiss.

Gianni recovered swiftly, snaking his free arm around Keelin's waist and hauling her even closer. He could taste the rage in her kiss and it infected his blood with an urgent need to dominate and seduce.

He moved his hand up her back and caught her hair in his fist, tugging her head back gently, but just enough so that she had to ease the pressure on his mouth. And as soon as he had that tiny space, he took over, coaxing her to open to him, sensing her resistance but using every trick in the book.

When he felt resistance give way and those lush lips open under his, the sense of triumph was faintly disturbing. He shouldn't be feeling so buoyant just from a kiss. But there was something about this woman giving in to him, even as minutely as this, that made him ridiculously triumphant.

Gianni was aware on some dim level that they were in a room full of people whose opinion mattered to him, but he couldn't seem to care. All he wanted to do was wrap both arms around Keelin and plunder her mouth until he was drunk on her scent and taste. Until he could taste *all* of her.

He finally broke the kiss and drew back, looking down at her. It took a long second for her to open her eyes and when she did they were dark green and filled with depths and lights that made Gianni want to push her away. Fast. But he couldn't. They were being watched. And now their appreciative crowd was clapping and cheering.

Every provocative curve of her body was imprinted against him and he cursed silently, furiously willing his body to cool down for fear of people seeing just how undone she made him feel.

'I've been looking for you for the past thirty minutes.'

Keelin whirled around from where she'd been standing on an empty terrace just off a quiet garden courtyard in the hotel, seeing but not seeing the amazing view of Rome at night laid out before her.

Her head was still too consumed with that

kiss and how effortlessly Gianni had shown his dominance, *again*. As soon as she could she'd escaped, feeling far too claustrophobic, as if a net was tightening around her. And hot, needing air to cool down.

She raised the hand that still held her clutch bag. 'Well, now you've found me.'

He said in a low voice, as if mindful they might not be totally alone, 'I don't appreciate being ambushed in public.'

'That's rich coming from you!' Keelin said with reproof, still vibrating angrily from that explosive kiss. Not that she could even blame him!

She turned her back to the view. 'And what do you call staging that party and inviting my parents if not an ambush?'

Gianni's bow tie was undone, his top button open—as if he'd done it with impatience, looking for her? She tried not to notice how dark and gorgeous he was against the lush backdrop of the hotel garden.

He narrowed his gaze. 'Seeing you with your parents certainly was interesting.'

Keelin tossed her head and batted away the vulnerability. It wasn't her fault her parents didn't love her, even though she'd not truly believed that for a long time. They were just supremely selfish people who never should have had a child.

'Believe me, they'll be only too happy to wash their hands of me and hand me over like some kind of medieval chattel. Does that make me a little less palatable?'

He smiled but it was hard. 'Not in the least. I won't have to endure interminable in-law dinners with them.'

His obduracy pushed Keelin over an edge. She threw up her hands. 'This is crazy! We should just call it off here and now. It'll never work.'

'That's the problem, you can't call it off and I won't,' Gianni pointed out calmly enough to make her frustration increase. 'It'll work just fine. You'll have everything you could possibly need. I'll make sure you're happy.'

Keelin stalked forward, quivering with anger. 'You wouldn't have the first clue about what might make me happy but I'll give you a hint— you're nowhere near the vicinity of that picture.'

She was shocked to find herself feeling so agitated and hated it. It reminded her of the futile rage she'd felt growing up that had ended up in bids for attention and she was damned if she was going to let this man induce it again. She forced herself to calm.

Gianni's voice had an edge. 'You know, I think I preferred it when you were vacuous and shallow.'

Something awfully like hurt gripped Keelin

inside. 'Most men would prefer that easier option, my father certainly does. And tell me,' she asked in a rush, 'where exactly will I fit into your life—presumably while you're off building your empire?'

She put up a hand. 'Wait, don't tell me—I'll be tied to a bed, awaiting your return for the next bout of conjugal rights?'

Gianni folded his arms, making muscles bunch. Keelin hated being so aware of him.

'I've never indulged in bondage before,' he drawled, 'but I'm certainly willing to give it a go. I hear it's the *in* thing.'

To her shock and horror, an image popped into her head of Gianni on his back, naked, with his arms tied high above his head, as she straddled him and bent down, her hair trailing over his chest, mouth watering at the prospect of tasting his skin—

She abruptly shut down that very rogue thought and blurted out hotly, 'You're impossible. This whole situation is impossible.'

'Like I said before, there's nothing stopping you from walking out the door, Keelin. I'm no gaoler,' he pointed out unhelpfully.

She made a *pfft* sound. 'As if you'd let me thwart your chances now.'

Gianni shrugged and gave all the appearance of being at ease but she could sense the tension in him. 'I'm sure I can find a deal to achieve global distribution elsewhere, but not with half the kudos that O'Connor's can bring me, so no, I won't let you thwart my chances.'

In a fit of angry frustration, Keelin turned back to the view, aghast to feel the prickle of hot tears. *Dammit.* She would not let this man make her cry.

'You looked happy in the photo in your father's office.'

Keelin blinked and went still, surprised as much by the abrupt change of subject as the fact that Gianni had noticed that photo.

Slowly she turned around again, crossing her arms tight across her chest. 'What did you imagine, Gianni? That the picture was taken by a loving father indulging his daughter in her favourite activity?'

She answered herself. 'As you've seen this evening, that's hardly the case. That picture was taken on a hacienda in Andalusia. I went out there one summer with a schoolfriend—' She just stopped herself in time from saying, *Because my parents were too busy to spend time with me*, hating the moment of self-pity.

'One of the trainers took the picture. When my father saw it on my phone he insisted he get a copy of it. It's not in his office as a tender reminder of his daughter. It's there because he likes to promote the myth that we are a normal loving family.'

Gianni's face was inscrutable. 'What was it about the horses that you liked so much?'

Now Keelin felt even more exposed. 'Why do you want to know?' she asked tetchily.

Gianni sounded almost weary. He ran a hand through his hair. 'We need to get to know each other, Keelin.'

Her immediate instinct was to deny this but then something of his weariness and the futility of this whole situation crept into her system and the urge to fight seemed to dissolve away, treacherously.

She avoided Gianni's eye and shrugged minutely. 'It was the first time anyone gave me responsibility for something. Proper responsibility. They needed an extra pair of hands because one of their grooms was taken ill.'

She looked up, but Gianni was still expressionless. It made it easier. 'I stayed at the stables with the grooms, in the most rudimentary of accommodation. When we weren't working with the horses and exercising them, we helped with picking the vines for the harvest. I'd never worked so hard. I don't think I knew what work was until then and it made me realise that I could be of use, that I had the ability to make a difference, work within a team.'

What she didn't say was that those were the happiest days of her life, living so simply and freely. For once not thinking of some new way to make her father notice her. Even though, when he found out what she'd been doing, he hit the roof and dragged her back home. He wouldn't let her into his world, but he also wasn't going to see his daughter doing dirty work. Her mother had been disgusted. She'd gone conker brown and had calluses all over her hands.

Then Gianni said, 'I spent some of my summers picking vines too.'

Keelin's heart lurched. 'You did?'

He nodded. 'I used to go back to Sicily with my grandfather to help pick vines for his oldest friend. That's where I learnt everything there is to know about wine.'

'Oh,' Keelin said a little lamely, finding it hard not to think of a young Gianni stripped to the waist, olive skin gleaming with sweat and muscles moving sinuously as he worked.

'I mean it, Keelin.' He said softly now, 'I will build you a hacienda and fill it with horses if that's what will make you happy.'

Before, this statement might have incited her to rage, but now she felt as if he'd soothed something inside her. Dangerous. He was just using another tactic to get her where he wanted.

'I want to work, Gianni. I want to be counted.

I want a place on the board of O'Connor's, my rightful place. *That's* what I want, and I don't think it fits in with your idea of a dutiful wife.'

His mouth firmed. They were back to square one. 'I have to admit that it isn't exactly how I envisaged things but that's not to say that we can't discuss it. I want you to be happy, Keelin.'

She knew without pursuing it that Gianni might concede her some kind of Mickey Mouse position just to placate her. She'd been too inured by her father's ways to trust that once they were married Gianni would give her any power at all. She realised then that she'd lost the ability to trust in any man giving her what she wanted.

She hated that she'd revealed herself to him now. She'd never told anyone about how important that time in Spain had been to her. She felt exposed.

'You don't get it, do you?' Her weary tone matched his. 'I can buy my own hacienda and fill it with horses if I so wish, but I'll do it on my terms, with my own hard-earned money. I'm still going to do everything in my power to see that this marriage falls apart.'

'That's the annoying thing though,' Gianni said with deceptive mildness. 'I've no intention of this falling apart.'

CHAPTER FIVE

KEELIN KNEW THAT Gianni meant what he said. He would do whatever it took to get her up that aisle and then firmly sequester her somewhere out of the way while he got on with amassing power and a fortune, exactly like her father. Even though, for a second, she'd caught a glimpse of another side of Gianni. One that she never would have expected to feel empathy with.

He unfolded his arms then and checked his watch. 'Much as I'd love to stay and chat, I have some international calls to make.'

He was backing away, leaving, and to Keelin's horror she felt a lurch, as if all the cells in her body wanted to go with him. She took a step back.

He stopped then as if he'd just thought of something. He said silkily, 'Oh, and I should let you know that I've decided to bring our wedding forward by a week, to capitalise on the success of this evening.'

Shock took a second to reverberate through her system. Her mouth opened. She'd been a fool to consider a mutual feeling of empathy for a second. He was ruthless to the bone. 'Can you even do that?'

Gianni smiled but it was infinitely mocking. 'With my underground connections? I can do what I like. So by this time next week we'll be man and wife, Keelin.'

Her arms were so tight around herself that she was almost stopping the blood flow to her upper body. She forced out sarcastically, 'Your eagerness to marry me is truly personally flattering.'

Gianni's smile turned enigmatic. 'I wouldn't be so cruel as to pretend otherwise for a second.'

And with a brief hard smile, he turned and left the garden, disappearing through overhanging foliage. In a fit of delayed anger—why was it that her reactions which were usually so crystal-sharp felt more sluggish around Gianni?—Keelin made an inarticulate sound of frustration and turned around again, the view doing little to soothe her. It mocked her, as if to say, *Why can't you just be happy with this?*

She looked down then and saw Gianni emerge confidently from the main hotel entrance just below. Instinctively she moved closer to the terrace wall so she could see better. His driver jumped out to open his door for him but at the last second Gianni stopped and said something to him. He pulled off his jacket and threw it into the car and turned and walked off, hands in his pockets, broad shoulders slightly hunched, head down. Dark and formidable against the mild early-summer Roman night.

Keelin drew back a little, almost as if he might turn and look up at her, catch her staring.

Curiously, her anger defused slightly. She found herself wondering why he'd decided to walk. Was he having a fit of conscience? Wondering if he really could go through with a marriage of convenience to someone who hated him?

And did she hate him? She hated this situation she was in. But she had to admit that in other circumstances she would find Gianni intriguing, and far too dangerously attractive. He was so composed. Controlled. And ruthless. Something roiled inside her to think that after all she'd been through, some part of her psyche resonated with powerful ambitious men like her father.

And then she had to realise that by pursuing this dogged and crazy plan, she was doing nothing less than exhibiting her own ruthlessness and ambition. The fact that she embodied those traits, too, did not sit well for a moment.

A very rogue image slid into Keelin's mind; of

her, coming out of the hotel behind Gianni and slipping her hand into his. And of him turning to look down, a smile on his face. The kind of easy smile that she'd seen him bestow on people all night at the party but not her. Because when he looked at her it was always with a mix of mockery, disdain or anger. But maybe he'd stop this time and turn and put his hands around her face and there would be a different look in his eyes—

What the hell was wrong with her?

Keelin whirled away from the wall with enough force to make her stumble slightly. She was breathing heavily, her heart racing. Damn Gianni Delucca. What was she doing mooning after him like some kind of groupie, forgetting about the bombshell he'd just dropped?

Keelin went back up to her suite, and once inside, she kicked off her heels and paced up and down, restless at the thought of the wedding happening in a few days. She had nothing to hide from Gianni any more. They were on a level playing pitch now, so as far as she was concerned, nothing had changed and it was still very much *game on* to derail this wedding and she would utilise whatever arsenal she could lay her hands on to achieve this.

As if the universe wanted to help her, Keelin noticed the front of the local newspaper that was delivered to her suite every day. It featured a colourful picture of a famous celebrity leaving the rival Chatsfield Hotel in Rome.Keelin's mouth curved into a smile as an audacious plan took root in her head.

As Gianni approached his apartment and office building after walking from the Harrington Hotel, he still felt restless. And he knew it wasn't just the pent-up lust in his system. He still wasn't quite sure how he'd kept his hands off Keelin after that incendiary kiss at the party. And just now? She'd looked as mad as hell and sexy with it. Her vibrant red hair tumbled over one pale shoulder. Cheeks pink, mouth still slightly swollen from that kiss. Green eyes flashing when he'd imparted the news of bringing the wedding forward, a mutinous set to her jaw.

Knowing how determined she was to get out of this marriage, Gianni had decided to bring the wedding forward, telling himself it was purely a strategic business move.

So why had he had to steel himself inwardly and call on the kind of ruthlessness he employed when making a tough business decision when he'd told her? Because when Keelin had confided in him about her time in Andalusia, it had impacted him on a level he hadn't expected. He'd been able to see that fresh-faced image of her all too easily and it was a million miles from the kind of woman he might have believed her to be, even without all the fake tan and blingy jewellery.

And the fact that she always seemed so ready to fight, to rebel, had impacted on him too. Gianni had the strong and uncomfortable feeling that life for her had been one battle or another for a long time. He didn't like how that made him feel, almost protective.

So he'd had to push all that down. Be remorseless. For all he knew, it was a sob story, concocted to appeal to his sympathies. Although something about the reluctance with which she'd told him made it ring true. And now he couldn't get that image of her smiling face out of his head.

But he had to. Because she would be upping her game now and pulling out every trick in the book to try and sabotage this wedding and Gianni would be the biggest fool on the planet if he didn't suspect as much and act accordingly.

'Miss O'Connor, are you sure that Signor Delucca has agreed to this?'

Keelin smiled sweetly. 'Oh, yes, my fiancé has given me carte blanche to make all the arrangements and he really doesn't expect to be bothered with questions. You can leave all that to me.'

The nice wedding planner, Allessandra, looked at Keelin a little doubtfully but then smiled too, and said confidentially and not without a little relief, 'In all honesty I find Signor Delucca quite intimidating.'

Keelin patted the girl's hand. 'I understand completely, so it's better this way.'

It was two days before the wedding and Keelin had finally pushed Gianni so far with a never-ending list of questions about the arrangements that he'd texted her the previous day and said succinctly, Do what you like, Keelin. I don't care if you turn up in a clown's outfit on Saturday afternoon as long as you're there. G.

So she had taken his words to heart and was calmly and diligently wreaking a little havoc with everything Gianni had ordered for the wedding.

The first thing to go had been the wedding dress he'd apparently chosen for her. She'd taken one look at it and felt a betraying hitch in her breathing. Because if she had one uncynical bone left in her body, one tiny atom left where she harboured any kind of romantic dream of marrying a soul mate, then this was the dress she would wear.

It was elegant, off-white. Strapless with an unstructured sweetheart neckline, it hugged the breasts and torso before falling in delicate folds of chiffon to the floor. Whimsical and romantic.

So naturally, she'd chosen another, altogether far less suitable dress. Not that she had any hopes he'd actually *see* her in it. But it would be enough that she might be photographed in it to add to the furore.

She'd barely seen Gianni in the past few days because he'd been busy with meetings. This suited Keelin fine. She was still suffering from sudden and random memory flashes of the rough and smooth slide of his tongue against hers as he'd kissed her senseless in front of everyone at the engagement party. And she couldn't even blame him!

She pushed down the niggle of her conscience as she made the most drastic changes to the wedding yet, and told herself that she was doing this for her very survival.

Gianni cursed volubly when his cufflink slipped free for the third time while trying to close it.

Dio.

He stopped and took a breath. What the hell was wrong with him? Anyone would think he was having traditional bridegroom jitters! For what was in all essence just part of a business merger.

Part of a business merger that was happening

today. He'd been reliably informed that Keelin O'Connor was in her hotel, apparently making her own preparations. And that she hadn't fled the country.

Perhaps she was hoping that he would balk at the final hurdle? The reality of marriage a little too much to take? And in truth, he did feel slightly constricted at the thought but not enough to jeopardise everything he'd worked so hard for. It had more to do with her effect on him, that lack of control he felt around her.

The cufflink finally slid home and Gianni gave himself a critical once-over in the mirror. Dressed in a dark grey morning suit with a light grey silk cravat tie, he was the epitome of sartorial elegance, but for once he didn't feel that measure of satisfaction at another sign that he was removing himself from his past.

He felt uneasy now that he'd allowed Keelin to needle him enough to give her carte blanche to organise the wedding arrangements. He'd assured himself that she couldn't get up to too much trouble right under his nose, could she?

For someone who never doubted his instincts, Gianni pushed aside the concern and flicked a glance at his watch and cursed himself again. He was ready too early for the afternoon ceremony. Like some kind of besotted fool? No, he assured himself, he just wanted to get this wedding over with so that he could get on with merging forces with O'Connor.

This urgency he felt was purely for that, nothing else.

When someone knocked on the door of his apartment he welcomed the distraction, opening it to reveal his assistant, looking scared and holding a local tabloid paper. The young man cleared his voice. 'Have you spoken to Miss O'Connor today?'

Gianni immediately went cold. 'No. Why?'

His assistant handed him the paper, where a blazing headline read *Delucca's Fiancée Snubs Harrington in Favour of Chatsfield for Lavish Wedding Ceremony!*

It took a long second for the news to sink in. Keelin had gone behind his back and changed the venue, capitalising on the very public rivalry between the hotel dynasties to generate as much adverse publicity as possible.

Gianni forced the swell of rage down and said grimly, 'Get my driver and car.'

The assistant rushed off, only too happy to get out of Gianni's dark angry orbit.

Keelin would not get away with this. But first, it was time to go and make her his wife.

'Well, where the hell is he?'

Keelin tried to curb any sense of obvious excitement at her father's increasingly angry questions as to the whereabouts of her apparently absent fiancé.

She was light-headed at the audacity of what she was doing and she quashed the niggle of her conscience when she recalled the injured looks and feverish whispering she'd left behind at the Harrington Hotel after telling them she was moving the wedding. But it had been too good an opportunity to miss. Gianni had clearly favoured a discreetly elegant affair at The Harrington with the emphasis on discretion, and so Keelin had seen an opportunity to turn the wedding into a far more publicly opulent and luxurious extravaganza, much to The Chatsfield PR's delight, always eager to score points where possible and take the focus off The Harrington's latest venture—an ice bar in Russia which was all over the papers because it was being created by billionaire Lukas Kovach.

It also just so happened that one of Keelin's oldest school friends from her junior boarding school in Ireland was Orla Kennedy, who was now married to Antonio Chatsfield, the scion of the Chatsfield family, so one phone call was all it had taken to unleash a little carnage.

Where forty guests *had* been expected, over a hundred now jostled for space in The Chatsfield's sumptuously decorated ballroom. There were enough flowers to open a shop.

'Well?'

Her father's voice and the low rumble of voices from the ballroom next door made her snap back to attention. Keelin tried to look worried. 'I don't know, Father, maybe he's had second thoughts.'

Her conscience twinged. *Or maybe Gianni is completely unaware about the latest developments thanks to her blithely informing everyone that he'd sanctioned the changes and didn't want to be bothered about the minutiae.*

Her father went pale and Keelin's gaze narrowed on him. Did he really care that much? But before she could interpret that nugget, a knock came on the door and Allessandra the wedding planner stepped into the room.

The woman had been looking almost sick with anxiety before, but now her face was wreathed in smiles and Keelin barely had a chance to suspect the worst when she said with clear relief, 'The groom has arrived. You should take your places.'

Keelin could feel the colour leach from her face. *No.* This isn't how it was meant to go. She'd deliberately made sure everyone *but* Gianni was aware of the location and earlier time change. And right about when everyone would be feeling sorry for the jilted bride, he'd be realising far too late what she'd done. Too late to do anything but appear to have stood her up.

But he was here.

She was barely aware of her father taking her arm in a firm grip and saying, 'About time. I knew he wouldn't bail.'

Keelin was in too much shock to see the colour return to her father's face. The *Wedding March* was playing, the guests had gone quiet. Someone pulled her veil over her face and pushed a bouquet into her hands. And then the door opened and her father propelled her forward.

Gianni felt Keelin arrive alongside him in front of the registrar for this civil ceremony. He was still too angry to look at her but he turned his head eventually and his eyes widened at the sight of her. A shot of lust went straight to his groin.

He didn't know why he should have expected her to be wearing the elegant wedding dress he'd picked out, but he still wasn't prepared to see her in a tight lace sheath of a dress that ended somewhere around her upper thighs, displaying those long bare legs to perfection.

Sheer sleeves and a lace neckline above the bodice was almost laughingly demure when every provocative curve of her body was lovingly outlined by the material.

Her hair was down in sleek red waves and a short veil covered her face but he could see through the gauzy material that she was pale and looking straight ahead. Something caught the corner of his eye and he looked down to see her hands in a white-knuckle grip around the bouquet, fingers trembling ever so slightly.

Gianni recognised that she was obviously in shock that he'd thwarted her plans, so with a quick nod to the celebrant he urged him on, knowing he needed to take advantage of this moment. He ruthlessly drove down any concerns about the evident lengths Keelin had gone to to signal her reluctance for this union. He'd narrowly averted a PR disaster but he was here now and he would deal with his errant wife afterwards.

Keelin was walking back down the aisle, her mouth still tingling from Gianni's hard kiss with her hand tucked firmly in his arm, before she seemed to come out of the slightly nightmarish paralysis that had gripped her ever since she'd realised she hadn't succeeded in derailing the wedding.

Everyone was clapping as they walked into a lavishly laid-out ballroom for the wedding reception/lunch. But Gianni veered away from the waiting staff and guests, saying curtly, 'Give us a minute please,' and took Keelin's hand, all but dragging her over to a doorway which led into a little anteroom.

He pushed her in ahead of him none too gently and came in behind her, shutting the door. Keelin turned to face him, legs wobbly from shock, and a delayed surge of adrenalin. Had she really just repeated vows to this man? And signed a register? Like some kind of pathetic automaton?

Gianni was livid, and somewhere it registered uncomfortably into Keelin's mind that she felt a kick of excitement to see him after the few days of little or no contact.

His accent was thicker than she'd heard it before. 'Did you imagine that right about now you'd be playing the part of the poor jilted bride crying crocodile tears while the local rags drooled over the salacious headlines?'

Keelin opened her mouth but clearly he didn't expect an answer.

'If your acting was going to be anything like the performance you subjected me to when we first met, then they would have seen through you in seconds,' Gianni said with derision dripping from his voice.

Keelin's own anger at having sleepwalked

through her worst nightmare finally broke through the shock and she gesticulated wildly with the hand holding the bouquet. 'Well, *you* didn't! So I might just have got away with it.'

Gianni's mouth tightened. 'You won't be walking anywhere now except out of this hotel with me, as man and wife.'

He reached for her free hand and held it up to face her so she could see the platinum band of her wedding ring glinting mockingly under the lights. And then he held up his own hand, displaying the matching ring. 'See? For better or worse, *mia moglie.' My wife.*

The sight of those wedding bands side by side gave Keelin a jolt and it wasn't one entirely of disgust. She'd always vowed not to be like her mother, married to a man just for the sake of security. Yet here she was, married, and she couldn't seem to drum up the appropriate sense of rage. Gianni was scrambling her responses. And her brain.

But before she could make sense of that, he cupped her jaw, a look of unmistakable determination on his face, voice rough. 'The sooner we consummate this marriage and make it real in every sense, the better.'

Keelin immediately felt breathless, a rush of excitement zinging straight to the cluster of nerves between her legs. She gritted her jaw. No

way was he going to have her flat on her back
and exposing all of her vulnerabilities to his blis-
tering gaze. She still hid so much from him, not
least of which was the fact that she was innocent and had a very real fear of a man making
her feel powerless, and threatened. 'Dream on,
Delucca. I will not be sharing your bed.'

He just smiled. Infuriatingly confident. 'I
wouldn't be so sure about that.'

And then with dismayingly easy strength he
slid his hand around to the back of her neck and
tugged her towards him, his other arm going
around her waist to draw her up against his rock-
hard *aroused* body.

To find him so ready, in the midst of this
heated exchange, made Keelin burn. A giddy
rush of instant desire rose up in answer to his
body's question. She wanted him too, and the
knowledge mocked her. Where was the fear
now? She'd lie down all too easily for this man,
that was the problem, in spite of what had happened to her.

'I thought I told you already. I have strong
moral views and this will be a marriage in name
and practice.'

Keelin opened her mouth to object even if
her body wouldn't but the light was blocked and
her mouth was covered by the firm contours of
Gianni's lips, moving expertly, enticing. For a

betraying few seconds, her entire being cleaved to his, her mouth clinging, tongues tangling passionately. And then, somehow—she wasn't sure how—just before she lost any ability to stay clear, she bit down on his lower lip, making him pull back abruptly with a crude curse.

When she saw the droplet of blood and his tongue snake out to touch it her insides tightened with remorse. If he knew how innocent she really was, he would laugh his head off.

'I meant it, Gianni.' She felt shaky, and wasn't sure what she really meant any more.

He licked away the blood, his eyes dark. And she found it hard to focus, or remember why she'd bitten him.

'And I meant it too, *gattino*. You shouldn't display your claws unless you're prepared for the consequences. As much as I'd like to prove you wrong here and now, I refuse to let you reduce us to such baseness with a hundred guests waiting on the other side of this door. Another time perhaps.'

He took her hand and opened the door and then stopped dead. Keelin couldn't see past him because his big frame blocked the doorway, and then he rounded on her so fast her head spun. If she'd thought he'd looked livid before then, now his rage was infinitely worse.

'And who the *hell* invited my father's old cronies?'

Keelin's blood drained south and she swallowed. It had felt like a risky thing to do when she'd thought of it but she'd ignored her conscience when she'd decided to make contact with Gianni's mother before the wedding.

'I, er, mentioned something to your mother about being sure to welcome anyone she wanted to invite.'

Gianni's eyes were so black now they looked like cold obsidian, and all that heat had been replaced by ice. Keelin suppressed a shiver. She really didn't know this man or what he was capable of, although she did trust implicitly that he wouldn't hurt her. Not physically anyway. Even if he did look as though he wanted to throttle her right now.

'Don't you ever use my mother like that again, got it? You leave her out of this vendetta against me, Keelin.'

The clear warning ringing in his voice rendered her a little mute as something went tight in her belly, to recognise his protective streak and know that the last person it would ever be directed towards would be *her*.

A few interminable hours later as guests finally began to depart—his mother being one of the first as she hated leaving her home unless it was vitally necessary—Gianni was still seething with a mix of anger and mounting sexual frustration.

How dared Keelin use his mother just to score a point off him?

When he'd properly registered who the extra guests were, his blood had almost boiled over to see those familiar old faces from his father's past, battered and bruised, hardened by the lives they'd lived and the things they'd seen.

Silly to think he'd felt a measure of complacency in believing he was far enough removed from them by now, but no. It had been like getting a cold blast of water in his face. He'd almost heard his father's mocking laugh and rough voice in his ear: 'So you're too good for us now, heh?'

He could also see the headlines undoubtedly being run up at that very moment: *Delucca's Wedding Brings Out Familiar Faces... Like Father Like Son After All?*

Gianni was mildly relieved to note that thankfully most of his father's friends had left by now.

But the person who had subjected him to this very unwelcome scrutiny was still very much here and on the other side of the room, talking very energetically to a group of rapt-looking guests.

Keelin had studiously avoided him from the moment they'd emerged from the anteroom. Even while eating, she'd been practically sitting in the lap of the person beside her, rather than talk to him.

Wherever he'd moved, she'd gone in the opposite direction as if they were made of opposing magnets, when Gianni knew that was anything but the case. Just before she'd bitten his lip earlier, he'd felt her body tipping over the edge, softening, curving into his. She wanted him.

And he wanted her with a hunger made more intense by that edge of anger. It might have concerned him at any other time, but he couldn't seem to take his eyes off her sleek curves in that ridiculous dress. His hands itched to take it off and devour her until something of this ravenous beast inside him was slayed. He felt rough and raw, the reminder of the past far too close for comfort.

Making his excuses to the people around him, Gianni strode across the room to his wife. Her back was to him but he saw her stiffen minutely just as he came alongside her and took her hand in his with a firm grip.

Predictably she tried to break free but his grip tightened. He smiled urbanely even as he battled to keep his libido and body under control, just for a while longer. Until he could be alone with this biting *gattino* and tame her once and for all.

The guests melted away with knowing looks and smiles. Keelin turned to Gianni. She still wore the veil even though it was slightly askew. She held a glass of wine in her hand and her cheeks looked suspiciously flushed.

He took the drink and put it down, saying stringently, 'I don't like women who drink excessively in public.'

Keelin hissed, 'Well, then maybe you shouldn't have married me. It's never too early to start divorce proceedings, you know.'

Gianni straightened up and looked at her and something in his chest tightened. She wasn't drunk, he could see that. She looked beautiful. Angry, but stunning. Green eyes huge and mossy. Mouth ripe for kissing. And he intended to. But not here.

He curbed his libido. Soon—within a matter of hours—she would be under him and finally giving him the first sense of satisfaction and peace he'd had since he'd agreed to this whole thing. With the anticipation of that carnal satisfaction snaking through his blood and taking some of the edge off his anger, he said, 'There will be no more talk of divorce. It's time to go, *mia amata*.'

Immediately she tensed. 'Where?'

Lust tightened his body in spite of his best efforts and fired up his blood. He smiled. 'On our honeymoon, of course. I can't wait to get you all to myself.'

CHAPTER SIX

WITHOUT EVEN GIVING her time to change, Gianni bundled Keelin, veil and all, into a waiting limousine outside the Chatsfield Hotel, accompanied by the inevitable flashes of the paparazzi cameras. They pulled out smoothly into the Rome evening traffic after Gianni had taken his seat in the back.

She had been avoiding him and that simmering rage all afternoon like a coward. Every time she'd looked at him she'd just seen those black eyes and the banked fire in their depths, and could still feel the firmness of his lip between her teeth all over again. And the guilt to have been audacious enough to encourage his mother to invite those people, especially when the meek and mild woman had said nervously, 'I don't know, Gianni won't like it.'

So now she felt doubly guilty. When she was the one who had been marched up the aisle. *So why didn't you just turn and run?* asked a snarky inner voice. Keelin ignored it, that feeling of in-evitability and how she'd succumbed to it, too vivid for her liking.

She only realised then that she was still, ri-diculously, holding on to her bouquet. She said a little redundantly now, 'I should have thrown it.'

Gianni plucked it out of her hand and pressed a button so that his window slid down. A group of female tourists were standing on a corner reading a map near where the car was stalled at a red light. Gianni shouted out, *'Signora!'*

They looked up and Keelin could see their collective double takes as they took in who was calling to them and she could have rolled her eyes. But then he was calling out, 'Catch!' and he lobbed out the bouquet which flew high into the air and then into one of the girl's outstretched hands. Much to her squealing delight.

Gianni didn't respond, he just hit the button and the window slid back up again. Keelin's mouth had opened in shock. He looked at her as the car moved off again, a mocking glint in his eyes. 'Is it not traditional for the groom to throw it?'

Keelin shut her mouth and then said icily, 'No, it's not. But then not a lot about this wedding is traditional.'

'Don't worry,' Gianni growled softly, 'I have

every intention of this marriage becoming very traditional very soon.'

Her breath shortened at the explicit look in Gianni's eyes. 'We have to talk about this. You can't seriously expect that we're going to just—'

He cut her off. 'I do seriously expect that this marriage will be a real and enduring one, Keelin, so the sooner you come to terms with that, the better.'

She crossed her arms over her chest and was aware of how ridiculous she must look. Angrily she ripped the veil off her head then, wincing as pins caught in her hair. She shrank back when Gianni hissed his disapproval and put out a hand as if to help.

'It's fine. I can do it.'

She continued to pick out pins and said angrily, 'Since when did someone like you ever want to have a *real* and *enduring* marriage?'

Gianni's anger matched hers. 'Since it came with a business deal that will make Delucca a brand name all over the world and a wife who I want more than any other woman.'

Keelin was fired up and ready to blast back with a response but her words dissolved on her tongue. *A wife who I want more than any other woman.*

And just like that she could feel something crumble inside her, give way. Treacherously. She dragged her gaze away from his long enough to notice that they were driving into an airfield where a helicopter was waiting.

'Where are we going?' she asked, avoiding thinking about what he'd just said and how it made her feel.

Gianni seemed to curb his anger. 'We're going to my villa in Umbria. For a week. It's remote enough to keep you out of mischief and it's where we can really get to know each other and start our happily married life together.'

The fact that his words held a sarcastic edge made Keelin feel stupid for having lost her focus for a second.

'Does it have a tower?' she asked tartly. 'So you can lock me away and just call this marriage what it is—a prison?'

He tutted and smiled a little. 'Such a dramatic imagination. Bondage, imprisonment, whatever will you think of next?'

Keelin wanted to launch herself at him across the back of the car and wring his neck but he was opening his door and stepping out of the car before she could do anything. The driver had opened her door and was waiting solicitously for her to get out too.

She eventually did, huffily. Still clutching the veil. Gianni was lifting two small suitcases out of the boot and carrying them over to the helicopter where a pilot was waiting. Keelin followed, reluctantly. 'What about the rest of my things?'

Gianni threw back carelessly, 'They've been sent on ahead.'

She muttered something under her breath about hoping he'd remembered to pack the hair shirts. When she caught up with him at the helicopter he turned and said dryly, 'I wouldn't dream of marking your skin with a hair shirt, Keelin. You'll dress in nothing but silk and satin, for my delectation.'

She scowled at him, not liking the way she had a sudden urge to see the expression on Gianni's face if she *was* to parade before him in some sensual silk concoction.

'Neanderthal.'

He just smiled but behind it Keelin could see the remnants of his anger. He still hadn't forgiven her for almost derailing the wedding. Or for engineering the invitation of his father's henchmen.

He held out a hand and she looked at it warily. Gianni's smile faded and he said crisply, 'It's a long walk back into Rome in a short wedding dress and high heels, Keelin.'

Giving in to the inevitable, she slapped her hand into his and let him help her up and into the aircraft. He buckled her in, big capable hands moving far too close to her belly and breasts with proprietorial ease. As if she was already his. She might be in name, but not in the way it mattered most, deep in her body and soul. And she vowed then that he would never reach that part of her. At least then she'd have rights to sue for divorce on grounds of nonconsummation!

Gianni took the veil out of her hand. 'I don't think you need this any more, do you?'

He didn't wait for an answer, just put it somewhere in the back with the bags. The pilot joined them, climbing into the front, greeting Keelin warmly and not looking remotely fazed to have a petulant-looking bride for a passenger. Gianni shut Keelin's door and then he swung into the other seat at the front and handed her some headphones. 'Put these on.'

She took them and smiled faux sweetly. 'Yes, sir.'

It was only when she saw him communicate with the pilot and flip some switches that she realised that Gianni was co-piloting the helicopter. The rotor blades were whirring now and any grudging admiration she might have felt went south with her belly when the small craft lifted off the ground with a wobbly tilt and then into the dusky sky.

When Keelin had got over her white-knuckle terror of being on her first helicopter ride, she looked down and could see Rome spread out beneath her. Gianni's voice came into her headphones. 'Look down to the right, you'll see the Colosseum.'

Keelin did, and sucked in a breath. It was so beautiful, already illuminated in floodlights for the early evening. Gianni proceeded to point out other landmarks and Keelin was struck dumb by the experience, and also because he was being so solicitous.

He stopped the travelogue when they were clearly leaving Rome behind and she felt absurdly buoyant after the experience. She had to force herself to look away from the back of his dark silky hair and broad shoulders. He'd just been polite, that's all. But she wouldn't have expected it of him after the roller coaster of the day.

The problem was, for a small moment Keelin had almost fooled herself into thinking that they were a couple heading off on a romantic honeymoon, for real. And it hadn't felt all that disturbing.

By the time they were landing Keelin's knuckles were white with fear again. It was too dark now to really make out the surroundings. The helicopter touched down with a small bounce, and when the engine was switched off and the blades had stopped turning, the silence was almost deafening.

Gianni was opening her door and Keelin's mouth went dry. His short hair was tousled and his tie was undone, the top button of his shirt open. He held out a hand and after a moment Keelin let him take hers, feeling those long fingers wrap tight around her.

He said goodbye to the pilot and was leading her over to a jeep parked nearby. After putting bags in the back, he got into the front beside her and she saw that keys had been left in the ignition. Clearly they were on his private estate.

Feeling seriously intimidated she asked, 'Where are we exactly?'

Gianni was focusing on driving along a rough path. 'We're not too far from a town called Montefalco, south of Perugia.' 'Oh.'

They came to a halt outside the entrance of a grand-looking villa. The door opened and light spilled out along with the figure of a petite older woman dressed in black. Gianni got out and greeted her with warm kisses on both cheeks. She was already taking the bags off him and he called something out to her as she went back inside. She laughed in response and it made Keelin's hackles rise as she could well imagine Gianni had said something about *his wife*.

She hated not knowing what they'd said and

found herself making a vow to learn Italian before she stopped herself—what was she thinking? She wouldn't be married long enough to need Italian!

Gianni came around to the passenger door and she was out before he could touch her. The old woman was back now, without their bags.

Gianni said, 'Keelin, meet Lucia Cabreze, who runs the villa.'

Innate good manners made Keelin move forward to accept the hand she was offered and she smiled. No need for this woman to suffer because she hated Gianni.

He explained Lucia's apologetic expression. 'She doesn't speak English but she hopes you'll be happy here. I've assured her you will.'

Keelin smiled back and tried to indicate the same sentiment while shooting Gianni a filthy look.

Then the woman stood back and made a shooing gesture for them to go inside. No doubt so that there could be no further delay in getting down to the business at hand.

Keelin yelped when Gianni dipped and she felt herself being lifted into his arms. 'What are you doing?' she gritted, her heart pounding shamefully at this over-the-top masculine gesture.

Gianni, not remotely out of breath as he

climbed the steps, said easily, 'Lucia will expect it, she's traditional. And don't you know it's an ancient Roman custom to carry brides over the threshold because they're not meant to be happy at leaving their father's houses? So they had to appear to be all but dragged into their new homes.'

Keelin huffed inelegantly as Gianni climbed an inner set of stairs. 'Well, this is wrong on both counts, so you could have saved yourself the bother.'

Gianni was striding along a dark corridor now and he said, 'The other advantage is that it gets me where I want you that bit quicker.'

He finally put her down outside a door and opened it to reveal a vast suite bathed in soft romantic lighting. A huge four-poster bed dressed in lush dark red sheets was the focal point. It was a room for sensual abandon. A room for lovers.

Keelin turned around and came face to face with Gianni's chest. She looked up and could only see the stark and determined lines of his face. Her gut turned to jelly. He put his hands on her arms and slowly walked her backwards into the room, kicking the door shut behind him with a foot.

Her heart was thumping, blood racing. 'Gianni, please, we should talk about this.' She winced inwardly when she recalled her words: *I've been with, like, tons of guys.*

He took his arms off her and moved into the room, saying curtly, 'Funnily enough, I'm done with talking.' He pulled off his jacket and threw it down on a chair, a hand reaching up to his cravat.

Keelin gulped.

'Don't just stand there, *mia moglie*, take off your dress.'

When she didn't move he just said coldly, *'Now.'* He tore off his cravat and started on the buttons of his shirt to reveal his magnificent chest bit by bit, and panic gripped Keelin in earnest. He was so *masculine.*

When his shirt was half open he made a sound of frustration and irritation deep in his throat and abandoned undoing more buttons to stride over to Keelin.

Black eyes raked her up and down and he said throatily, 'Do you know what this dress has done to me all day?'

Keelin shook her head, fascinated by the intensity in his expression. He reached out and traced the lace edging that sat against her collarbone. Her breath hitched and her nipples went stiff against the material. Her hands felt sweaty.

'This dress has kept me on the very edge of my control. You wore it deliberately to provoke me, didn't you? Even if you did harbour the somewhat misguided hope that you could actually avoid marrying me.'Maybe,' he said now, musingly, 'I should have tried reverse psychology with you from the start? If I'd sent you this dress to wear, then you might have worn the other one, but you know what? I prefer this, because this dress is all about one thing—the only thing I'm interested in right now.'

Feeling dazed, and mesmerised, conscious of Gianni's finger moving back and forth seductively under the neck of the dress against her skin, she just said faintly, 'What's that?'

He looked at her, black clashing with green.

'*Sex*, Keelin. I want to make love to my beautiful wife.'

And with the most gentle yet deliberate of movements he brought his finger down the center of her dress, and the delicate lace ripped apart like butter melting either side of a hot knife until he got to the top of the bodice under the lace, just above her cleavage.

Then his other hand came up and with both hands he tore the lace edging away completely from front and back, so now Keelin stood before him in a strapless sheath of a minidress, with the remains of her sheer lace sleeves still on her arms. She might have appreciated the sartorial edginess of the look if she wasn't engulfed in shock and heat.

Gianni looked down at her, seeing her breasts barely confined by the bodice. For a moment she had a vision of him ripping that clean apart too. The fact that she wanted him to make love to her was a revelation that she couldn't really wrap her head around. How had it come to this so quickly? And yet she knew that if she had a choice right now, she wouldn't walk away. She was burning up inside and only he could assuage that.

She also had a keen sense of just how far she'd pushed him this time. He was clearly not in a gentle mood. And even though a part of her felt excited at his passion, another more sensible part knew she had to tell him the truth.

Her voice was shaky. 'Gianni, wait, there's something I should tell you.'

They were way beyond games now. Here was a bristling alpha male demanding his mate, and Keelin knew from the bulge in his trousers that she'd been aware of all day that he was more than ready to take her to bed. And while a part of her thrilled at that and ached for it too, she couldn't. Not like this. She wasn't experienced enough for him in this mood.

He bit out, 'Keelin, so help me, *Dio*.'

Fear fluttered along Keelin's nerve endings

dousing her desire. 'The thing is, I haven't been entirely honest.'

He was silent for a long moment and then he emitted a curt unamused laugh. '*Honest? Principessa*, you wouldn't know honesty if it jumped up and bit you on the ass.'

Keelin stung at that and she curled in on herself, inwardly. This man hated her. He was only marrying her because she came with a pass to unlimited business growth and potential. And here she was quivering before him like a virgin on their wedding night. *Well, that might be because you are a virgin*, a voice pointed out.

Gianni wrapped two hands around Keelin's waist, hauling her into his hard body. His hard, *hot* body.

'*Bella*, I know exactly what you are now. An amoral spoilt little liar who seeks only to get her own way, but I've won this round and now it's time for my prize and I'm going to claim it before I die of frustration.'

Then his mouth was on hers, hot and hard and demanding and so ruthlessly passionate that it scrambled every one of Keelin's functioning brain cells. Every corner of her body wanted this in spite of what her head was telling her about going slowly.

It was only when she felt his hands come to the zip at the back of the dress that some sanity broke through. She pulled her mouth away and pushed both hands against his chest. Hard. *'No.'*

Gianni looked at her. About to explode. Fingers poised to undress her completely.

'We need to stop, you need to stop.' Her mouth felt swollen. She backed away, dislodging his hands, and sucked in a deep quivering breath. 'The thing is that I've never done this before. I'm a virgin...'

Gianni just looked at her. Disbelief was etched onto his face. And then other expressions followed: derision, disdain and disgust. He backed away too.

Humiliation made her skin prickle to know she'd laid herself so bare for his ridicule. 'Gianni, wait, I—'

He put up a hand. *'Basta.* I don't want to hear it, Keelin. I've had enough of your lies and play-acting. Just go to bed. Damn you.'

And then he turned around and walked out, the door closing with incongruous softness behind him. Keelin looked at it in the gloom for a long time before reaction set in and she started to shake. The slivers of lace on the floor mocking her.

Her mind mercifully went to some numb place, induced by shock, fatigue and an overload of emotion. Vaguely aware of what she was doing, she kicked off her shoes and found the zip at the back of the dress, yanking it down. She stepped out of it and went to the bed, and climbed into it, pulling the luxurious covers over her body. And then she weakly shut out all of the voices and recriminations and slept.

When Keelin woke in the morning it took her long minutes to figure out where she was and why she was in her underwear in the most sumptuously soft bed she'd ever lain in.

Then she opened her eyes and took in the room and it all came flooding back, along with the reality of opulent dark red furnishings and antique furniture.

She came up on her elbows and looked around. The curtains hadn't been drawn so she pushed back the covers and got out, squinting a little at the daylight outside. A robe was behind the bathroom door, so after splashing some water on her face she pulled it on.

There were French doors and a balcony so she opened the doors and stepped out. The view took her breath away. Undulating green hills as far as the eye could see. For a moment she felt absurdly homesick as it reminded her of Ireland.

And then a low but powerful noise impacted—and she realised that that must have woken her up. And just as she thought that, she saw the helicopter rise up from the back of the property and bank to the left before disappearing off into the horizon, quickly becoming a small black dot. She hadn't been able to see who was in it but she assumed the pilot was taking it back to Rome.

Something skated over Keelin's skin to think of Gianni and how angry he'd been last night. And of facing him this morning. Recalling the events of the previous day felt a little dreamlike. Had it really happened?She looked down and saw the enormous diamond of her engagement ring and the slim wedding band.

Oh, yes, it had happened. She'd exchanged vows with the man in front of witnesses. And even now she could recall the strange kind of paralysis that had gripped her.

Knowing she'd have to face him sooner or later, Keelin went back inside and found that her things that had been sent on ahead were hanging up or in drawers. Along with a lot of clothes that looked brand-new. Her blood boiled slightly to think of him instructing someone anonymous to pick things out for her.

After a quick shower she dressed in worn jeans and one of her favourite plaid shirts and thought to herself that if Gianni didn't like it, then he'd have to get used to it because this was the real her.

But as she found her way downstairs she had

the uncanny sensation that Gianni wasn't *here*.
And until now she hadn't even realised she'd
been so aware of his whereabouts at any given
time.

Lucia the housekeeper appeared as Keelin got
to the bottom of the stairs looking a little worried. She spoke fast and made some kind of gesture with her hands, as if something was flying
away. It was the unmistakable concern mixed
with pity in her kind brown eyes that sent the
knowledge into Keelin's gut.

Gianni had been in the helicopter. He'd gone
somewhere and left her here. For a second she
almost couldn't breathe. Her belly lurched. Lucia
was taking her by the arm, still speaking unin-
telligible Italian, guiding Keelin to a gorgeous
outdoor terrace where a table was set for breakfast.

Lucia fussed around her but Keelin was
struggling to compute what that might mean, if
Gianni had left. Mechanically she ate what was
put in front of her and drank hot strong coffee.

She didn't like the awful creeping sensation of isolation, of being somehow powerless.
She was in a villa in the middle of nowhere—
it seemed—with not a word of Italian and no
idea why Gianni had left or when he'd be back.

She tried to ask Lucia if he'd left a note but
Lucia just shook her head, clearly not under-

standing. Smiling at Keelin apologetically, she seemed to make some more motions as if to say that Gianni would return.

When she'd bustled off again, Keelin decided to try his office in case he'd left a note there, but there was nothing but blank paper.

She sank down into his chair. Maybe this was it? She'd pushed him so far that he'd just left her here? So why didn't that evoke some sense of satisfaction or triumph? A kind of hysteria bubbled up but she pushed it back down. But she couldn't stop the edges of panic from gathering in the wings, ready to pounce and drag her back to her childhood.

Telling herself that he must have left momentarily and that there had to be some explanation, Keelin got up and forced herself to explore the villa. It was only when she returned about an hour later after having seen not another soul that the panic started to grip her in earnest.

Lucia couldn't be found now. It didn't even occur to Keelin to try and phone Gianni. He'd given her that card with his numbers when they'd met but she had no idea where it was now. And in any case her mobile phone battery was dead and she couldn't find her charger.

She was entirely alone in this vast villa somewhere south of Perugia and as the day wore on with no sign of Gianni returning, Keelin wasn't in Italy any more. She wasn't twenty-three. She was back in her past, at some indeterminate age, and she knew that there was not one person in the world who cared remotely where she was. Or that she was alone.

And slowly, the walls that she'd so painstakingly built over the years started to crumble, because she'd sworn she'd never allow this to happen again.

As Gianni drove back to the villa late that night the anger he'd been feeling all day was still there. His eyes were gritty from fatigue, and frustration pounded like a pulse in his blood.

Damn her. His wife, who he should have bedded last night. *His wife*. He'd almost been tempted to stay in Rome for the night but some very unwelcome sense of guilt had stopped him. Even though *he* shouldn't be feeling guilt.

When he thought of Keelin now though, all he could see in his mind's eye were the lurid images from last night, and how feral he'd felt as he stood in front of her. How badly he'd wanted to just rip that dress apart completely, baring her to his gaze.

And then Keelin had spouted the latest lie from her pretty mouth. A virgin. Ha! Virgins were as extinct as the dodo as far as Gianni was concerned. He'd stopped believing in virgins right about the time that the sixteen-year-old girl he'd been in love with had said to him patronisingly, 'Don't worry, I'll be gentle. It's your first time, isn't it?'

The memory faded...last night he'd felt as if he was climbing an interminable mountain. He'd also felt raw and exposed in his desire for Keelin when she kept pulling back, denying her own desire. A shudder of disgust went through him, to have been reduced to something almost mindless. Again. It had been enough to make him leave, get some space.

He cursed softly as he drove into the forecourt of the villa. No lights shone. Irritation surged, along with a sense of panic at the thought that Keelin might have gone. Disappeared.

A faint sense of unease prickled over his skin. He got out of the jeep and went up the steps, opening the door, flicking on a light. There wasn't a sound. But somehow Gianni sensed that she was here and something eased inside him, even as that irritation remained.

He took off his jacket and made his way up to the bedroom. It was dark up here too, and for a moment Gianni thought Keelin might be in bed asleep but then he saw a shape by the window.

He flicked on a light and Keelin was illuminated sitting in the window seat, legs drawn up under her chin, hair long and wild around her shoulders. And just like that, lust gripped him with a force that almost made him sway.

But something wasn't right about the picture. She wasn't moving. Gianni came further in. Feeling afraid now and not liking it, he rapped out, 'Keelin?'

Slowly she turned to look at him and he sucked in a breath at how pale she was and how huge her eyes looked. And as he watched, she seemed to come back to life, emotion making those eyes flash and burn like bright jewels.

She got up from the seat and came straight over to him, and lashed out, landing a blow to his chest before he could deflect it. It had enough force to make him take a step back.

'Don't you ever, *ever,* leave me alone like this again. Do you hear me? *Never.*'

Gianni stared at her. The anger in her voice was palpable. She looked haunted. Not piqued that he'd left her for a day. Haunted.

He said slowly, 'I would have thought that's exactly what you wanted since the day we met.'

CHAPTER SEVEN

KEELIN MIGHT HAVE agreed with Gianni if being abandoned wasn't her particular pyschological demon. Sensations were rushing into limbs that had been locked tight for hours, giving her shooting pains and pins and needles. Her hand throbbed from where she'd hit him. His chest was like a steel wall.

And worse, emotion was rising. Just to see him again. He'd come back. Damn him.

'You said nothing.' Keelin was accusing. 'You didn't even leave a note.'

Gianni's jaw tightened. 'I thought Lucia would tell you.'

Keelin let out a short harsh laugh. 'Via sign language? I don't speak Italian and she doesn't speak English.'

'You could have phoned me.'

Keelin felt a kind of shame wash over her. She'd slowly become more and more paralysed as the day had gone on. How could she explain that when one was in the grip of something like a panic attack, the last thing you did was the logical one?

'I couldn't find your number, and my phone was dead,' she supplied weakly. And then stronger, 'There was no one here. Even Lucia disappeared after a while. I was *all alone*. Anything could have happened, did you think of that?'

Irritation crossed Gianni's face. 'For God's sake, Keelin, it was only a day. You are in one of the most luxurious villas in Italy. There's an indoor pool and an outdoor pool—'

Keelin whirled away from him and the suggestion she should have been happy to amuse herself, emotion reaching her eyes, making them sting. Making her chest hurt with the pressure it took to contain it. She'd not cried in years, learning that tears only caused her parents to look at her with bafflement. So rousing their ire had become her default position.

Gianni sounded exasperated. 'Look—'

She kept her back to him and cut him off, saying with a low voice, 'When I was fourteen I got a taxi home from the train station for my summer half-term holidays. The whole house was locked up. When I rang my father he was in Sao Paulo in Brazil and wouldn't be home for days. My mother was in St Barts with friends. They'd given the staff a week off. They'd not even bothered to find out what I was doing.'

She turned around to face Gianni, arms folded tightly. 'They had to send the housekeeper back to take care of me and she was not happy to have her holiday cut short but at least it wasn't anything new so she wasn't surprised.'

Gianni interjected in a tight-sounding voice, 'This had happened before?'

Keelin lifted one shoulder in a gesture of assent. 'It was a fairly regular occurrence except usually there'd be staff at home. When I was three they left me alone with my nanny for two and a half months while they went to America on business. When they came back I didn't recognise them.'Today...' Emotion tightened her chest again but Keelin forced out, 'Today, it just got to me. It's isolated here. I don't speak the language. I *hate* that it affected me. But I just—don't do it again.'

Gianni came closer, all traces of exasperation and irritation gone. In his eyes was not pity, because Keelin couldn't have handled that. But something else. A kind of understanding.

He cupped his hands around her face, and it was only when he smoothed his thumbs back and forth across her cheeks she realised that she was crying. Mortification rushed through her and she tried to take his hands down but he wouldn't let her.

She'd planned on being icy and dismissive when he returned and instead she was blubbing all over him and spilling her guts. Keelin said, 'Look, it's not a big—'

He cut her off. 'I shouldn't have left you here with no explanation. The truth is that I was still angry after last night and I took it out on you by leaving you to go to Rome today. And the reason no one is here apart from Lucia is because I gave the staff a week off in a bid for some privacy. Today is Sunday so Lucia goes to her family in the local village for the day and night.'

Gianni's mouth was a tight line. 'It was careless and rude of me.'

Keelin's heart flip-flopped. *Uh-oh*.

And then he changed the subject abruptly. 'Have you eaten today?'

Keelin thought about it for a second and shook her head, feeling mortified again. Imagining he must be thinking, *She's such a drama queen*. 'Not since breakfast.' 'How about we get something to eat then, hmm?'

Keelin looked at him. 'Okay.'

He stepped back and took her hand and led her out of the room. All of Keelin's anger was washing away, to be replaced by something far more disturbing.

When they got down to the huge open-plan and surprisingly modern kitchen, Gianni directed Keelin to sit on a stool while he prepared pasta with a pesto sauce. Even though Keelin could see that he wasn't exactly making pasta from scratch, he seemed to know his way around a kitchen.

He poured her a glass of red wine and when she took a sip he said dryly, 'I take it that you *do* like wine?'

Keelin flushed and put the glass down, answering a little sheepishly, 'Yes.'

Gianni had rolled his shirtsleeves up, and taken his tie off, and even though he wore smart trousers, this was the most relaxed she'd seen him since they'd met. The open top button of his shirt drew her eye to the strong column of his throat. His jaw was dark with stubble. Keelin thought of him being angry enough to go to Rome that morning and sensed that he didn't normally let things provoke him to that extent. The realisation that she'd got to him made her feel somehow hollow though.

He looked at her as the pasta cooked, his gaze incisive. 'I'm also guessing your views on children and boarding school were not entirely accurate?'

She met his gaze. She guessed she deserved to give him an answer after stringing him along.

And she was passionate about this. She shook her head. 'No child of mine will ever go to one of those places.'

Gianni quirked a brow and instantly looked younger and even more devilishly handsome. 'Care to revise any more of your opinions?'

Keelin grimaced slightly and took another fortifying sip of wine before gesturing to her shirt and jeans. Bare feet. 'I've always been inclined to dress down more than up. And,' she admitted sheepishly, 'I hate shopping with a passion.'

But before he could probe any further and already feeling far too exposed, Keelin asked, 'What about you? You always seem to be so composed, pristine.'

Heat fizzed in her belly at the thought of what Gianni might look like completely undone. *Naked.*

Thankfully he was dishing up the pasta now and indicating for Keelin to go to the table, so he wasn't looking at her too closely. He put the plates down, brought over the wine. When Keelin tasted a mouthful of the perfectly *al dente* pasta with pesto sauce she closed her eyes for a second in appreciation. It was simple and rustic but it was heaven.

When she looked again, Gianni was taking a sip of wine, eyes unreadable, on her. Awareness made her self-conscious. She'd almost forgotten what she'd asked him when he said, 'Almost everything I do, and am, is a direct result of wanting to be the exact opposite of my father.'

Keelin remembered the way he'd retreated so spectacularly when she'd mentioned his father before, and his rage when he'd seen those men at the wedding, and kept silent.

He swallowed some pasta and put his fork down. Keelin couldn't seem to stop herself focusing on those lean hands. He spoke again, distracting her.

'My father was rough, tough, uncivilised. He got in with the wrong people at a young age in Sicily, and believed that the way to getting ahead was via violence and terrorising people, including my mother. I needed to prove to myself that I could be different.'

A million questions flooded into her brain but she sensed that Gianni was already regretting saying too much as he looked away and ate some pasta. She ignored the questions and said, 'Your mother seemed nice, quiet.'

Gianni grimaced slightly. 'She is. And she refuses to leave our old home just outside Rome. When my father died, I thought she'd move back to Sicily but she won't. She insists on keeping our home like a shrine.'

He shook his head and Keelin could understand that he didn't get why a woman who had been brutalised by her husband would want to do that. And it surprised Keelin too, but on some level she could understand that Gianni's mother perhaps still felt a sense of loyalty, and even love. After all, look at how far she herself had gone in a bid to prove something to her father after a lifetime of disinterest.

Quietly, before she could lose her nerve, she said, 'I'm sorry about what I did at the wedding, encouraging her to invite those men. I had no idea.'

Gianni looked at her and just inclined his head before smiling a little wryly. 'I can see how tempting it must have been to maximise a PR disaster.'

Keelin winced, but then he was saying, 'I've asked my mother to move here as I know she'd love it, but she won't.'

'It is beautiful,' Keelin offered, and he looked at her, surprised. She responded to his look with a dry, 'You know, if you're into that isolated bucolic crumbling idyll.'

He grimaced slightly as he pushed his empty plate away. 'It *is* isolated. Which is why I love it, but I never thought about what it might be like for someone else.'

Keelin felt a bit light-headed and knew she couldn't put it down to the wine, as she'd only had a drop. There was tension crackling between them but it was different to the tension she'd come to recognise. After all, things were different—they were married, so Gianni had won this round. But in that moment, Keelin couldn't seem to rouse herself to care all that much.

All she could see was the powerful man lounging just feet away from her, full of latent danger. And suddenly all she could think about was how he'd ordered her to take off her dress last night and how easily he'd ripped off the lace. And how badly she'd wanted him to rip off the dress.

She needed to explain. 'Look, about last night—'

He put up a hand, cutting her off. 'It's just us now, Keelin. No more lies, or acting, okay?'

She sat up straight, protesting hotly, 'But I wasn't lying about—'

Cutting her off again he said, 'It doesn't matter, okay? Let's have a cessation in hostilities. For now.'

Keelin's heart thumped hard. *A truce.* She was irritated he wouldn't give her a chance to explain but at the same time she was feeling incredibly vulnerable and didn't exactly want to go into it. But she had to.

'No,' she said firmly, 'I need to tell you this.'

Gianni looked at her, exasperation clear on his face. Keelin couldn't be so close to him and think straight. She got up and moved away, standing with her back to the sink, arms folded. She bit her lip and then said quickly, 'I wasn't lying last night. I am a virgin. I've never slept with anyone.'

He straightened up, his mouth thinned. 'Have you forgotten what you told me? Are you getting your stories so tangled up now that—'

Keelin cut him off. 'I told you that to wind you up. Why would I lie about this? It's not as if it wouldn't become pretty apparent.'

The blood seemed to leach from Gianni's face. He stood up and shook his head, clearly not understanding. 'You're twenty-three, how is it possible?'

Humiliation coiled in her belly. 'I know.' She steeled herself. 'The truth is that something happened to me—it kind of put me off wanting to have sex with anyone.' *Except you.* The knowledge beat like a drum in her blood.

Gianni folded his arms. 'What happened?'

Keelin couldn't stay still under that black gaze. She started to pace back and forth. She stopped and looked at him and took a breath. 'When I was seventeen, I was in a boarding school in Switzerland—it was my last school.'

He frowned. 'The one you ran away from?'

Keelin exhaled. 'Yes, that's the one.'

She went on. 'It was a weekend and I'd snuck

out of school with some friends to go to the local town. We were drinking at a bar and a group of guys came over. We all paired off, but then the guy I was with brought me outside to a secluded spot.'

Keelin felt embarrassed now to remember how she'd hungered for the male attention. 'We were fooling around, just kissing, nothing heavy, and then some of his friends came out.'

Something in Gianni's face hardened. 'Go on.'

Keelin's hands were curled to fists by her sides. 'I thought he'd tell them to leave, but they were laughing and joking. I tried to go back into the bar to find my friends but one of the guys blocked my way.'

She spoke quickly now. 'To be honest I don't remember much of what happened next...they overpowered me pretty quickly. Tripped me up and held me down on the ground. Two held my arms and someone else had my legs. They pulled my top off, tried to undo my trousers.'

'*Dio*, Keelin.' He looked shocked.

'Nothing happened,' she said quickly. 'I screamed and kicked out. I got one of them on the jaw. A staff member heard me and found us. The guys ran.'

Gianni was disgusted. 'Animals.'

Something very vulnerable moved inside Keelin to have blurted all that out. 'In a way it made me grow up. After that I focused on getting into college and studying. I did self-defence classes while I was in college, so I'd never feel helpless again. But that's why I shut down for so long.'

Gianni crossed the space between them and Keelin's heart thumped heavily. Gruffly he said, 'Do you feel threatened by me?'

Stripped bare of her defences, intoxicated by his proximity and infused with a headiness to have unburdened herself like that, she just shook her head. 'No.'

Gianni reached out and his hand cupped her jaw, thumb moving lightly over her cheek. His touch was amazingly gentle and it further defused something inside Keelin. Everything fell away except here and now, and them. And the heat suffusing the air between them.

'Will you let me make love to you, Keelin?'

A giddy rush of desire almost knocked her over with its force. She'd never wanted anything so badly. If he'd called her his wife, or made some allusion to their situation, it might have jarred her out of the moment, but he didn't. And in truth, she didn't care about any of that now. She just wanted him.

Jerkily, she nodded her head. 'Yes.'

He took her hand and led her out of the kitchen, up through the house and to the bedroom. With every step it only felt more right to Keelin. She wasn't someone who believed in any kind of mysticism but she had the sensation that there was literally nowhere else on earth she was meant to be, except here, right now, with this man.

When they were in the dimly lit bedroom with the door shut firmly behind them, Gianni led her over to the bed and turned around. He looked impossibly tall and broad. Strong and powerful, and something very feminine within Keelin reacted to that.

He lifted his hands and started to undo the buttons of her shirt, the backs of his fingers glancing off her hot skin. When they were all undone, he pushed open the shirt and drew it off her shoulders and down her arms so that it fell to the floor.

She felt intensely self-conscious in just her lace bra and almost jumped out of her skin when Gianni cupped the weight of one full breast and said softly, 'You're beautiful.'

She looked up, but words died in her mouth at the look in his eyes. He was so intent. Focused. Desirous. Her nipples drew tight, aching for his touch.

'Gianni,' she said weakly, not even sure how to articulate her desire.

'Shh, I know. We'll take this slow.'

An absurd lurch of emotion made Keelin's throat tighten. She'd never have expected this of Gianni.

His fingers were on the buttons of his shirt now, but in a bid to drive down the emotion, Keelin said impulsively, 'Let me.'

His hands dropped and his eyes were hooded as she stepped closer and started to undo his buttons, revealing his broad chest bit by gorgeous bit. When she'd undone them all she pushed his shirt apart, over his shoulders and down his arms, just like he'd done to her.

Her eyes widened. He was truly magnificent. Not an ounce of spare flesh. A male animal in his muscular prime. Dark skin, lightly covered with hair, blunt nipples. And the enticing ridges of muscles leading down to his pants.

Galvanised by something she'd never felt before, Keelin brought her hands to his belt, undoing it and sliding it through the loops with a sibilant hiss. She let it fall to the floor. And then she was undoing the top button, the skin of his hard flat abdomen hot against her knuckles.

His hand came to the back of her neck and she looked up at him, only realising then that she was breathing hard, and sweating lightly.

Gianni pulled her against him and he was tugging on her hair gently to tip her face up. The hard thrust of his erection pressed against her belly and she wanted to move against it, but then his mouth was on hers and his hand was on her bare back, fingers expertly undoing the clasp of her bra and spreading out over her naked skin.

Their mouths fit like missing pieces of a jigsaw, welded together, tongues duelling, teeth nipping. Keelin's hands spread across Gianni's chest, fingers curling against his skin, nails scraping those blunt nipples, making him shudder against her. It was heady, intoxicating.

She was dimly aware of his hands moving to the straps of her bra and pulling them down—the scrap of material being tugged free from between them until her bare breasts brushed against his hot skin enticingly.

And then they'd stopped kissing and Gianni moved back slightly to look at her, that dark gaze glittering in the dim light. She felt self-conscious and wanted to bring her hands up. He stopped her. '*Dio*, you are so beautiful.'

He reached out and rubbed a thumb back and forth across one hard peak, making it harden even more, almost painfully. Stinging.

'Gianni,' she whispered, not even aware she was saying his name.

'Hmm?'

It was as if they were both drugged. Falling deeper and deeper into some sensual vortex.

He sat down on the bed but kept his hands

on her waist, bringing her with him so that she stood between his legs. She looked down to see his head come close and then his mouth closed over one tight peak, and she gasped at the intensely pleasurable sensation of his hot mouth and tongue suckling her, licking, biting gently.

Her legs wobbled and his hands tightened on her as his mouth wreaked sensual havoc on her other breast. She wasn't even aware of her hands on his head, fingers tangling in short silky hair, clasping him to her.

When he took his mouth away, she felt dizzy. His hands came to her jeans, undoing the button, pulling down the zip, pulling them and her panties down. She helped him by kicking them off, any hint of self-consciousness gone now. She just wanted to be naked, no barriers between them.

When he stood up, her hands went automatically to his trousers, to finish what she'd started. Pulling the zip down, feeling that provocative bulge of male flesh.

His trousers dropped to the floor and he stepped out of them. Now he was confined only by snug jocks and they did little to hide his potent masculinity. Acting on blind feminine instinct, Keelin reached out to touch him, running her fingers along his shape and length under the material of his underwear. He jerked against her touch.

Gianni hissed out a breath and she looked at him. His cheeks were flushed, the lines of his face stark with need, and she felt a flutter of trepidation, for a moment jarred back to the fact that she was an innocent. Then something eased inside her. He knew. He wouldn't hurt her.

Gianni was pushing down his briefs now, freeing his erection and then sinking down onto the bed and pulling her with him, so that she fell on top of him in a tangle of limbs. Six foot three of honed lean muscle was underneath her and around her and she couldn't think.

Her naked breasts were crushed against Gianni's hard chest, and then he moved so that she lay on her back. His thigh was between hers and the ache between her legs made her increase the pressure against him subtly.

He smiled. 'Impatient *gattino*.'

A hand smoothed over her breast, exploring its shape and firmness, cupping it so that her nipple was offered up to him like an enticement. Every nerve ending screamed for satisfaction as Gianni slowly lowered his dark head, not to her breast but to her mouth.

That wicked mouth teased hers first and then lower, leaving a trail of hot blazing marks all over her skin before the hot wet slide of his tongue explored her nipples again with a sensual laziness that did nothing to help keep her from the brink. She moaned and moved against him, silently pleading for more.

She couldn't find purchase anywhere, hands slipping and sliding over his taut flesh as she tried to hang on to sanity.

But Gianni was remorseless. His other hand explored down over her belly, fingers moving between her legs, making them part, before he cupped the heated moist center of her body and Keelin went still.

He lifted his head from the torture of her breasts. She was flushed, hot, aroused, impatient—it had been a long time since she'd orgasmed, and when she had before, it had been because of ineffectual teenage explorations, not this far more adult and carnal experience.

Gianni's hand was moving against her now, finding her slick heat and releasing it. Fingers slipping and sliding against her. Exploring her body with a thoroughness that made her back arch in a silent plea. Without even knowing what she was doing, her legs parted to allow him more access and his fingers were sliding inside her, moving insistently, winding a tension so tight in her body that she bit her lip and tasted blood with the effort it took not to call out.

'Come for me, *cara*, I want to see you lose yourself.'

With two fingers thrusting in and out of her body, his thumb exerting subtle but expert pressure on her clitoris, Keelin hadn't a hope. She came around his fingers, almost on cue, and was blinded by the dizzying sweeping rush of clenching pleasure as it tipped her over the edge and into his expert hands, her mouth blindly seeking his, arms wrapped around him as she sobbed it out against him, shaken to her core by what had just happened.

Gianni was engulfed in heat and lust so powerful that he shook with it. Keelin's body was still spasming powerfully around his fingers; he could feel her teeth biting into his shoulder and welcomed the brief sharp pain.

Her breasts were pressed against him. In truth he wasn't sure how he'd held it together this long. Even that first sight of her naked body had almost tipped him over the edge. She was Venus incarnate, perfectly proportioned, with generous curves. All woman.

The tension left her body, finally. She lay back, eyes slumberous, looking at him. Slightly dazed. For some reason Gianni's chest tightened.

'Okay, *gattino*?'

Sounding deliciously sated, she said with a little slur, 'What's that mean?'

Gianni smiled, aware that since the moment he'd laid eyes on this woman, even in her trashy incarnation, he'd had this vision somewhere in his head. He smoothed back some hair from her flushed face.

'It means *kitten*.'

She half smiled, shy, and it made his chest tighter. 'I like it.'

Gianni moved against Keelin now and her eyes widened when she felt his erection. As if answering a prayer he hadn't even been aware of articulating, one small soft hand tentatively explored him but with such a light touch that it almost killed him.

He gritted out, 'I won't break.'

She bit her lower lip and her hand firmed around him, holding him in a snug embrace. Something about her shy hesitation made fresh anger surge to think of those animals and how terrified she must have been, how horrifically it might have ended. He forced the ugly image out, wanting to erase it from her head as well as his.

He needed to be inside her now or he'd spill on the sheets and make a fool of himself. He reached for protection and gently pulled Keelin's hand away so he could smooth it on. When he was sheathed, he moved so that he lay between her legs, the tip of his erection against where she was slick and hot. He touched her there with his thumb, rousing her again, until her breaths were coming shorter and sharper, muscles tensing with pre-pleasure.

'I want you, *mia bella.*'

She looked at him and her eyes were huge, and she said simply, 'Yes.'

Something crumbled apart inside him. He'd never experienced a moment like this with a woman before. But before he could allow that revelation to sink in, he drove into Keelin's body and felt the most intense rush of carnal euphoria explode along every nerve end, until he realised that her face was pale with shock, and her muscles were clamping like a vice around him. There was also something else on her face—*fear*. And he had a sudden image of how he must look above her. Feral. Intimidating.

He pulled free and fought not to wince.

'No,' she said fiercely, determination replacing the shock on her face. 'Don't stop.'

Something in Gianni's chest tightened to see her bravery, when clearly this had to be bringing back some memories.

'It's okay, I'm not stopping. We're just going to do it a little differently.' He came down on his back and encouraged Keelin to straddle him. When her legs were either side of his hips and he could feel that hot centre of her body slide against him he had to clench his jaw tight for a moment.

She sounded incredibly vulnerable when she said, 'What are you doing?'

Her hands were on his chest and he put his on her waist. 'I thought this might make it easier. Just now, you were scared for a second, weren't you?'

He could see her bite her lip, loath to admit it, but then she nodded. 'A little, but it's okay. I know you won't hurt me.'

Gianni shifted and felt his erection rise against her buttocks and bit back a groan. 'This way you won't feel so threatened...you can control the pace.'

She looked deliciously tousled, hair tumbling around her shoulders. Subtly Gianni moved her up, so that his erection was between them. He could see when she felt it—when her cheeks flushed. The centre of her body was poised over him, pushing him to the very limits of his control.

And then, with some kind of innate feminine understanding of her body and his, she slowly slid down and took him inside her. He could see her wince when her body clamped around his thick length again and he soothed her with words in Italian and English, hands moving her slowly up and down so that gradually she took more and more, until he was past the resistance and he was buried so deep he saw stars.

They were both breathing heavily. And then slowly, Keelin started to move her hips in a sinuous exploratory rhythm. He could feel her body grow slicker, her eyes widen as pleasure registered, cancelling out everything else.

He moved easier inside her and it made him even harder. He pulled her down over his chest and her hands went either side of his head, her breasts moving against him with the thrust of their bodies. Sweat slickened their skin. Gianni brought a hand down and caressed her bottom, squeezing the flesh as he gave in to the urge of his body to hold her still so that he could thrust up, harder and deeper.

His mouth found Keelin's nipple and tugged it deep, making her moan. 'Gianni, I need—'

He drew his mouth away and looked at her face. Her eyes were glazed, cheeks flushed. Their bodies were locked in a relentless dance.

'What do you need?' His voice was hoarse with restraint and longing.'Oh, God, I need *you*.' The half-coherent plea made him clasp her close, driving his body even deeper. Their mouths met and clung as they both finally tipped over the edge and fell crashing and burning to the ground.

In the minutes that followed, arms wrapped tight around her, Keelin's head tucked into his neck, and still buried deep inside her, Gianni had the rogue and very disturbing urge to never move again, loath to break the connection.

Keelin had never known such an intense feeling of satisfaction. Her whole body was throbbing lightly as her blood flow finally slowed down to normal, along with her heart rate.

And she had also never known what it was like to truly connect with someone else—when he'd pushed past her resistance, she'd had the sensation that he'd pushed past something much more than the physical. And that moment when Gianni had recognised her momentary fear and had pulled her over him so that she was on top—it was all too huge to think about now.

They were still connected and when he moved from underneath her she had to resist an urge to tighten her thighs around him so that he couldn't pull free.

When he lay beside her, she was too languorous to move, and too cowardly to open her eyes.

'Did I hurt you?'

She couldn't *not* open her eyes now. How could he think that? It had been the most profound experience of her life. But somehow she knew he might not appreciate that. So she just shook her head and said huskily, 'No, you didn't hurt me.'

He smoothed some damp hair off her cheek. He smiled but she could sense a tension in his smile. 'Good.' He drew her close then and the soporific effects of lovemaking made it easy for her to shut out all the scary revelations of what this now meant for their relationship. Or wonder what the tension behind his smile meant.

And then he just said, 'Go to sleep, Keelin.'

And almost before he'd finished saying it, her body had grown slack against him.

CHAPTER EIGHT

GIANNI CAREFULLY UNWRAPPED his arms from around Keelin's sleeping form. Climbing out of the bed, he went to the bathroom, and after dealing with the protection, he washed his hands and risked a look at himself in the mirror. He almost expected to look somehow different, because he felt slightly altered.

But he didn't. It was as if someone had turned the world upside down, shaken it about and then put it upright again. Everything looked the same, but it was all subtly different.

Not wanting to analyse why, beyond the fact that it had been the most amazing sex he'd ever experienced, he went back out to the room and dragged some sweatpants from a drawer, pulling them on.

As if drawn inexorably, he went back to stand beside the bed and looked down at the prone figure of Keelin for a long moment. Already he itched to touch her again, taste her, feel her body climax around him. *Dio.* Next time he might even be able to wait until she came first.

He was still reeling a little from the fact that she really had been a virgin and what she'd told him about her traumatic experience. It had roused the kind of protectiveness he'd only ever felt for one other person—his mother.

One cheek was down on the bed, red hair tumbled and wild across the pillow. Her lashes created a dark shadow on her cheek and her mouth was in a little moue, as if pouting for something in her sleep. His body tightened to think of her pouting for him.

Resisting the urge to slide back in beside her, he left the room silently and went to his office. He made straight for the drinks cabinet, pouring himself some whisky, and took an indelicate gulp, hoping that the alcohol might burn away some of the after-effects of that strange feeling of not being in his own skin any more.

He'd been shocked to return from Rome and find her so upset. At first he'd thought it was just feminine pique that he'd left her alone—which he lambasted himself for now—but it hadn't been. It had been rooted in a far deeper and more traumatic place.

He'd known that there was little love lost between her and her parents but had had no idea it stemmed from such wilful neglect. Even now

Gianni could feel an ominous tightening in his chest. And *anger* at her parents.

This whole relationship was veering way out of control. He'd imagined something far more clinical and less complicated. A wife who would be content with his wealth and status. A wife who would enhance his public reputation. A wife who would be happy to be getting on with her own concerns, leaving him to get on with his.

A wife who wouldn't ever provoke hot emotions and an even hotter lust. Or uncharacteristic behaviour—like when he'd taken off to Rome, feeling the need to get away from her constant provocation.

Gianni didn't do high drama or hot, out of control passion. He'd vowed not to let his life be at the mercy of such vagaries after his experiences growing up, and yet here he was, brimming over with the kind of wayward feelings he thought he'd locked away after his father had died.

This marriage was a business transaction. And he had to remember that, and make sure Keelin remembered it too. She'd been a virgin, and the last thing he needed was to become the object of some romantic ideal because he'd been her first. He could never fulfil her in that way, physically yes, but not romantically.

* * *

When Keelin woke she frowned. She felt different somehow. Muscles ached. She was naked. Between her legs was tender. And then she remembered what had happened and a wave of heat washed over her. She opened her eyes. The arms that had been around her were gone.

Gianni.

The bed was empty. She felt a mixture of relief and something else she didn't want to identify, telling herself it wasn't disappointment. The faintest streaks of dawn lit the sky outside. She came up on her elbows, wincing slightly when her body protested.

She went to the en suite and looked at her face in the mirror. Her eyes were huge and a little bit dazed. Her mouth looked swollen. Her jaw was slightly red from Gianni's stubble. And that brought back the memory of him thrusting up, deep inside her. So deep that she hadn't been able to catch her breath for a moment.

She'd never known that sex could be so amazing.

She pulled on a voluminous robe from the back of the bathroom door and went back out to the bedroom and sat on the bed. Everything was coming back in perfect recall now. It hadn't been some torrid dream. She'd slept with Gianni. She'd told him she wanted him.

What also came back was that funny smile he'd given her. The tension behind it. And a wave of hot mortification washed up through her. She'd been a virgin. Totally gauche and inexperienced. She'd thought it was amazing. But to Gianni, it must have been the most boring lovemaking experience of his life.

It was even worse when she recalled his entreaties, the way he'd so patiently pushed her over the edge, and all the while he must have been regretting the moment he'd ever agreed to this marriage.

The fact that he'd been so tender only made it worse now. Keelin wanted to cringe but also wanted to see him immediately, and somehow make him believe that last night hadn't been as earth-shattering as it really had.

He wasn't in any of the other bedrooms and she hated that she immediately feared that he'd left her alone again. Then she went down the stairs and saw a sliver of light coming from under his office door, and something in her chest eased. She pushed it open and saw him, barechested, hair tousled, scowling at something on his computer.

He looked up and she saw the unmistakable way some smooth expression blotted out the quick flash of his unguarded response to seeing her.

She stood stiffly by the door. 'Hey.'

Gianni leaned back in the chair, displaying his broad chest without even trying. Keelin's lower body pulsed in reaction.

'Hey,' he responded.

She could see that he was wearing sweatpants slung low on his hips, and there was something intensely sexy about this undone Gianni. A little redundantly she noted, 'You're working?' *Because he couldn't wait to get away from her?*

'Just catching up on some things.'

He stood up then and Keelin's mouth dried. He'd woken her body from a deep slumber and she could feel it respond helplessly, firming, moistening. Her breasts felt tight, nipples hard, pushing against the thick material of the robe.

Gianni walked over and stopped just in front of her. 'How are you feeling?'

Damn him for being so solicitous. It made her even more sure that he had to have been bored rigid with his virginal wife.

She affected a nonchalance she didn't feel and said airily, 'Fine, just fine.' And then panic that he might see something of her tumultuous emotions made her say, 'I wanted to talk to you actually.'

He frowned and folded his arms, which only made things worse. 'Me too, you go first.'

Keelin was relieved. She didn't really want to

hear what he had to say before she got out her bit. She avoided his eye, focusing on a spot near his shoulder. 'Look, last night was good.'

A hand snaked out and fingers caught her chin, tipping it up. Those dark eyes were flashing now. 'Good? That's all you can say about it?'

Keelin felt as if someone had jerked a rug from under her feet. 'Well, what did you want me to say?'

Gianni let her chin go and stepped back, cursing softly. 'I would have thought it merited a description slightly more compelling than *good*. I felt you come around me, Keelin, you broke apart.'

She flushed and hated him right then. 'Well, maybe I did. Okay, it was good sex.' She threw her hands up. 'What would I know? It was my first time!'

He stalked closer, vibrating with danger, and growled softly, 'Believe me, *cara*, it was more than good, or great. I've never had sex like that.'

Now Keelin lurched to intense vulnerability; she hadn't expected this. 'You haven't?'

He shook his head. 'No.'

She swallowed, not liking the way this confession made her feel weak. 'Maybe it was just because I was a virgin?'

Gianni reached out and pushed one side of her robe aside to cup her breast intimately. Immediately her breath seized and fire licked through her veins. He shook his head again. 'Next time, it'll be even better. And all the next times, *mia moglie.*'

My wife. Now there was something triumphant in his expression, and acting on an instinct, Keelin slapped his hand away and yanked her robe back over her breasts. She felt way too exposed and raw after last night and needed to assert some sense of reality, before her see-sawing emotions made her forget reality entirely.

'Nothing's changed, Gianni. I still don't want to be here.'

His hand dropped and his face darkened. 'Do you ever stop fighting?'

Emotion made her chest tight. 'I don't think I know how.'

Gianni turned away from her as if sick of the sight of her when moments ago he'd been cupping her flesh, arousing her all over again. His back was smooth and broad, tapering down to slim hips. His sweatpants riding low. Keelin had to battle a rogue urge to move forward and press against him, sliding her arms around him.

He turned back and she flushed.

'Do you or do you not want to contribute to your family business?'

Keelin had to focus. Damn him for making her forget the most important thing. 'Of course my priority is O'Connor's but I shouldn't have to prove it through a marriage.'

Gianni came closer and looked intimidating, but she felt no fear. Only a need to stand up to him.

His voice was stern. 'You are my wife now, in every sense of the word.'

Keelin's hands grabbed the lapels of the robe, and she blurted out, 'Just because we slept together, it doesn't mean anything.'

Liar.

Gianni looked as if he might explode for a moment. That was probably one of the worst things you could say to a possessive Italian man.

She found herself asking, 'Why is it so important to you? This deal?'

Keelin thought he might not actually answer and then he ran a hand through his hair impatiently. For some reason the gesture tugged at her, as if she could sense a kindred sense of turmoil.

He looked at her. 'It's important because I want to atone for my father's actions, as well as create my own business.'

She frowned. 'What do you mean? It wasn't your fault he was the way he was.'

Gianni shook his head. 'I don't mean like that.' He sighed and continued with obvious reluctance, 'My grandfather, *his* father, set up our family business in Sicily before moving it onto the mainland, just outside Rome, to try and grow it. It was my grandfather's pride and joy, and a major achievement that he'd managed to get out of Sicily and make a life for himself and his son. His wife had died in Sicily.'

'But my father was a teenager by then and had already become involved with the Mafia in Sicily. He forged new links in Rome. When my grandfather became too ill to work, my father let the business run into the ground. He kept it going only to use as a front for his Mafia activities. It broke my grandfather apart. We were close.'

Keelin was sorry for asking now. She didn't want to know this about Gianni. She didn't want to empathise with him or feel sympathy. Especially not after last night's intimacies.

But he ignored her silent plea and she could see the steeliness in his expression. 'I've made it my life's ambition to reclaim what my grandfather set out to do, to create a family business we can be proud of.'

She tried not to let Gianni's story affect her. 'We're not so different, you know. We want similar things, but I have to give up what I want so that you can get yours.'

His expression became even steelier; as if to emphasise that, he folded his arms. 'I'm sorry about that, but I'm not prepared to lose this chance now, Keelin.'

Feeling desperate she said, 'You really are ruthless, aren't you?'

He didn't look remotely perturbed by that. 'Nothing will deter me from this course of action.'

He undid his arms and came closer. All she could see was bare chest. Dammit, now was not a time to get distracted by his physicality. She averted her eyes and glared at him, sure that he was fully aware of his effect on her and using it.

'You really want to leave here? Walk away from this marriage right now?'

Suddenly Keelin felt as if the wind had been knocked from her chest. She hadn't expected that. And far from feeling a resounding *yes* rising up within her, it was something much more ambiguous. But she forced out, 'Yes, of course.'

Gianni looked at her for a long moment and she could see some kind of struggle being waged behind those dark eyes and that implacable expression. He stepped back. 'Fine.'

She blinked and swallowed. 'What?'

His jaw clenched. 'You heard me. I don't want you to ever feel isolated or trapped here, Keelin. I'm not some gaoler. I don't relish the fact that your father attached you to this deal like some kind of medieval chattel but he did, and the fact is that aside from all of that, something unexpected has happened. Mutual desire.'

He waited for a moment, almost as if he expected her to deny it, but she couldn't. Not after last night.

'But one thing I won't grant you is a divorce and you know the reasons why. However, I'm not such a masochist that I'll live in a constant state of war because you're not mature enough to admit you want me, or to give this marriage a decent chance.'

She lashed out hotly, 'That's—'

But he lifted a hand and said coldly, 'Meet me back downstairs with your bag packed in half an hour.'

Keelin was still trembling when she zipped up her bag. Her belly had dropped somewhere around her feet when Gianni had told her to pack her bag. Worst of all was the awfully familiar sensation of being sent away. First by her parents, and now this. And she was *hurt*. It was slicing through her like a knife, making her bleed internally.

She sat on the bed for a second, her hair still damp from the shower, trailing down her back. What was wrong with her? Since when did Gianni have the power to hurt her like this? Since when would she not have jumped at a chance to regain her freedom? Even if he wasn't promising divorce, he was clearly prepared for her to get on with her life.

And then lurid images flashed into her head from last night. Two hearts beating in unison, biting his shoulder like some kind of animal, sweaty limbs sliding together urgently, the deepest connection—she closed her eyes desperately but that only made it worse. She opened them again.

Was Gianni right? Was she immature? Not looking at this like an adult? Still locked into acting out the part of the rebel that had been assigned to her so long ago that she followed it slavishly?

Was he really sending her away? No, she realised, he was giving her a choice. Asking her to stand up and ask for what she wanted.

Feeling incredibly insecure and hating it, Keelin stood up and took her bag in her hand. On her way down the stairs she half expected to see Gianni barring the door—maybe he'd been calling her bluff?

But when she saw him he was waiting, looking reserved but at ease, keys in his hands. When she reached him he took her bag, not saying anything, and led her outside.

She followed Gianni to where the jeep was parked. He threw her the keys and she caught them on a reflex. He answered her surprised look. 'I told you I'm not a gaoler, Keelin. You should get used to driving on the opposite side of the road, and get a feel for the jeep.'

Keelin got in and felt butterflies tie her belly in knots. Gianni was like a stranger. A polite, distant stranger.

Carefully she navigated out of the villa driveway and onto the open road, getting used to the left-hand drive. Gianni made her do a grand loop of the estate and she saw just how massive it was.

Then he was giving her different directions and after about fifteen minutes they drove into a small sleepy town.

'This is the closest town for basic supplies, and a train station.' He pointed. 'Park over there.'

Keelin dutifully pulled into a space. She killed the engine, feeling suddenly nervous.

Gianni took off his seat belt and turned to face her. 'One of my cars was delivered into town ahead of us. I'm going to drive it home.'

He glanced at his watch and then at Keelin, his expression completely inscrutable. 'There's a train to Rome in two hours. I'm going to leave you here now and you can decide what you want to do. You can be my wife in absentia, or you can own up to the fact that you want me too, and decide to try and make the best of this situation, *with me.*'

Keelin stared at him. There was no artifice any more. No game-playing. This was it. Straight up and unadorned. Gianni leaned over then and cupped her jaw with his hand. She felt faint calluses on his skin and her blood sizzled.

He came close enough to kiss her but stopped just short. The nerve ends in her lips tingled, as if pleading for his touch. With those black eyes locked on hers he said, 'I want you, Keelin, and I want you to stay. But I won't beg.'

And then he drew back, taking his hand away. He got out of the jeep and closed the door. Keelin watched him walk across the small street and get into a low-slung sports car. The engine surged to life, making her flinch minutely, and he took off without so much as a glance in her direction.

In the quiet aftermath came a sense of desolation far worse than the one she'd felt when she'd realised she was alone in the villa. Keelin wasn't sure how long she stayed in the jeep, still a little stunned, but eventually she got out and went to a small café and ordered a coffee. She saw people come into the town, clearly for the train, sitting in cars, and more came into the café with bags.

She cursed Gianni for giving her this choice. And at the same time she cursed herself because he was right. She'd been reacting to him from the moment she'd seen him and had taken little or no responsibility for her own actions. It was all so messed up. Why couldn't she have met Gianni outside of this crazy condition of her father's?

That inner revelation shocked her. To finally acknowledge with brutal honesty that she hated the circumstances which had brought them together. But she didn't hate the man. At all. He was the first man who had breached the formidable walls of her defences, without even trying very hard.

He was the first person she'd been completely honest with.

Was she so reluctant to deal with her own desires that she would have preferred Gianni to lock her in the villa and seduce her into some kind of mindless state where she could abdicate all responsibility for her own feelings and desires?

The train pulled into the station and there was a surge of people towards the platform. But Keelin didn't move. When Gianni had said to her earlier, *Do you ever stop fighting?* she'd answered, *I don't think I know how.*

She realised she was incredibly weary now. She'd been fighting for a long time. For love and attention. For recognition.

She didn't like to admit that something about

the fact that Gianni was prepared to admit he wanted her to stay, but was also prepared to let her go, made it almost impossible to leave.

She'd been seeking her father's approval ever since she'd become aware of his rejection of her because she was a girl. It had informed all of her actions, including her endless teenage searching for love via whichever boy would give her the tiniest bit of attention. Until that awful night had brought her to her senses and given her a delayed sense of self-worth.

And now she was in this situation and all of a sudden everything which had been so clear and clean-cut to her was blurry. The only thing in sharp focus was Gianni Delucca and this fire he'd ignited in her belly. She'd handed more than just her virginity over to him last night. She'd *trusted* him. And he'd restored a piece of her innocence that had been ripped away by those boys.

A very fragile flame flickered to life inside her. Perhaps this marriage wasn't a dead end? Or the loss of her independence? Maybe she could make Gianni see how serious she was about wanting a chance?

The whistle for the train sounded and Keelin jerked as if someone had pinched her.

This was it. She could run for the train and continue fighting, or she could stay and go back to that villa, and face Gianni and herself. As the train pulled out of the station, the inner revelation mocked her; there'd never been a choice. From the moment Gianni had been prepared to let her go, she'd wanted to stay.

When Gianni saw the dust cloud from his office window as the jeep came back down the drive, a tension he was unaware of holding on to left his body. The train would have left fifteen minutes ago and in spite of his sanguine attitude he'd been on the verge of calling for the helicopter to get back to Rome to meet the train on the other end.

It had been a gamble to give Keelin the choice of leaving. But when she'd kept insisting this wasn't what she wanted he'd had the sick realisation that he was no better than his bullying father if he forced her to stay.

He'd had an appreciation of just how he'd steamrollered Keelin into the marriage, giving her little or no room to manoeuvre. And while he certainly wasn't about to grant her total freedom, he'd also realised that he wanted her to *want* to stay.

The real Keelin O'Connor was proving to be far more enigmatic than he might ever have imagined. Revealing new facets all the time, like a true chameleon.

One thing was sure—she wasn't the malleable sweet wife he'd arrogantly assumed she would be when he'd agreed to marry her sight unseen, and she'd been punishing him for that from day one. Gianni knew on some level he deserved it, but also, he knew with a sense of disquiet that even if he had a choice, he wouldn't let Keelin go right now.

The jeep came closer—he could make out the red sheen of her hair, the pale oval of her face. His blood leapt as she drove around to the front of the villa and a new kind of tension came into his body. A far more carnal one. And then he went to meet her.

Gianni waited in the doorway, careful to keep his expression neutral, aware that it wouldn't take much to send Keelin fleeing again. She looked at him carefully when she came up the steps.

He just took her bags and said lightly, 'Lucia has prepared some lunch. Are you hungry?'

Keelin admitted ruefully, 'Starving.'

He held out his hand but before she took it she said, 'This morning, you said you had something to say to me too—what was it?'

For a moment Gianni had to think back. And then he remembered. He'd planned on gently letting her know that physical intimacy didn't equate to emotional intimacy. But she'd assured him pretty comprehensively that she was under no such illusions. And why didn't that mollify him now?

He just said, 'It was nothing important.'

She looked at him again for a long moment but then something cleared in those mesmerising green eyes and she took his hand, and Gianni wrapped his fingers around hers. He forced down a burgeoning sense of lightness and led her out to the patio where Lucia bustled around them serving up a delicious lunch and he initiated a conversation that came nowhere near the tumultuous events of the morning, or the significance of Keelin's return.

CHAPTER NINE

'WHERE ARE WE GOING?'

It was after lunch and Gianni was driving the jeep. He glanced at her and then back to the road. 'I thought it'd be good to get out, show you around a bit.'

Keelin rested her head back against the seat. For some reason she was perfectly happy to just wait and see where they ended up. Since she'd returned to the villa, a kind of weight had lifted off her shoulders.

She'd changed into a plain but pretty green sundress and the warm Umbrian air tickled her bare skin, the scent of grass and flowers heady. Gianni was wearing worn jeans, and a polo shirt, and every time Keelin looked at him she got a fresh jolt of lust, and surprise, to see him dressed down like this.

He said a little abruptly then, 'Where's your engagement ring?'

Keelin immediately flushed guiltily and looked

at her hand, bare but for the wedding band. 'Back at the villa. I, ah, forgot to put it on.'

He looked at her, eyes narrowed. 'It's not really you, is it?'

Keelin's belly somersaulted. 'Not really, no.'

He looked back to the road. 'I'll get you a new one.'

She shook her head quickly, disturbed by the thought of being presented with a ring she might actually like. 'No, it's fine. The wedding band is enough.'

Gianni sent her a dry look. 'A woman who won't accept jewellery?'

Keelin scowled at him but he took her hand in his and lifted it to his mouth, pressing a kiss against the back of it, making the pulse between her legs throb.

And then he said with a twitch to his gorgeous mouth, 'You're not like any woman I've ever met, Keelin O'Connor Delucca.'

The fact that those two names together didn't invoke revulsion was yet another blow against Keelin's armour of defences. Damn him.

A few hours later Keelin was huffing and puffing inelegantly as she followed Gianni up the hilly street in the stunning mountaintop town of Montefalco. When he stopped she saw that they were in a huge picturesque square. He truly was the quintessential Italian hunk, effortlessly drawing attention from women passing them by.

He turned and looked at her. 'Okay?'

Keelin felt flushed in the fading early-evening sunshine. 'Fine,' she said, more tetchily than she intended. Not liking how aware she was of other women's interest in Gianni.

He took her hand and tugged her with him across the square. 'We'll have dinner over here.'

They'd spent the afternoon looking around the dozens of stunning frescoed medieval churches in the town which Gianni had told her was nicknamed 'the balcony of Umbria' because of its spectacular views.

The small restaurant had fairy lights twinkling through the bushes that shielded it from the square discreetly. Pretty tables and chairs were under an awning. A tall man came out and greeted Gianni profusely with grand Italian gesticulations and appreciative looks in Keelin's direction.

They were led to a table that was both tucked away from the others and yet had great views of the rolling Umbrian plains. Gianni broke from his conversation with his friend to ask her, 'Do you mind if I order for you? There's some regional specialities you might like.'

Keelin shrugged as she pulled on a light cardigan she'd had wrapped around her waist. She was more seduced by this charming Gianni than she liked to admit. 'I'll eat almost anything. Except snails.'

She also didn't like to think of how close she'd come to being back in Rome, alone and feeling a hollow sense of victory.

An efficient waiter arrived within seconds and poured them water. Keelin took a thirsty gulp and looked up to see Gianni sitting back, staring at her. Immediately she felt dishevelled, self-conscious. 'What? Am I sweaty?'

He shook his head. 'You have no idea how beautiful you are, do you?' He leant forward. 'It's a rare woman who can go out without any make-up and yet put all the other women around her to shame.'

Keelin flushed. 'You don't need to say that—'

'I do,' he said simply. 'You're stunning.'

She was completely unused to getting compliments. Her mother had always despaired that Keelin was a redhead like her and had fought a constant battle to become blonder and blonder herself. She'd spent ridiculous amounts of money on hiding her natural Celtic freckles, and would tell Keelin ad nauseum about men who hated that au natural look she favoured.

She fiddled with her glass. 'Well, thank you.' She snuck Gianni a glance and said with a wry twitch of her mouth, 'You're not exactly ugly yourself.'

He put a hand to his chest in mock incredulity. 'I think that's the first nice thing you've ever said to me.'

Keelin dipped her fingers in her water and flicked it at him, her mouth twitching in earnest now. 'As if you need to be told.'

He leant forward again and said mock conspiratorially, 'All men are craving reassurance underneath their confident exteriors.'

The waiter reappeared with two glasses of white wine. He lifted his glass. 'What shall we toast to?'

Keelin's chest felt tight. *What shall we toast to indeed?* She lifted hers. 'The present moment.'

Those black eyes glittered, almost as if he could see into her head and know what the thought process had been behind her return to the villa earlier. He tipped his glass towards her. 'To us, Keelin.'

She took a quick sip. Her skin felt sensitive and whenever he looked at her she was acutely aware of herself. While they'd been looking around the town he'd taken every opportunity to touch her in small ways—taking her hand, touching her back, protecting her if a crowd of tourists jostled them.

She pushed aside the suspicion that Gianni

was merely going all out to do his best to seduce her into becoming the malleable wife he wanted. The cool wine slid like sweet tart nectar down her throat, imbuing her with a sense of deep relaxation, complicit in this indulgence.

And with the same skill he'd exhibited earlier, Gianni drew her into a light conversation. The fact that it managed to reinforce how much they seemed to have in common chipped away at yet more of Keelin's badly dented defences.

He sat back at one stage, a definite gleam of triumph in his eyes. 'You said it yourself, we're really not that different after all.'

Keelin wanted to scowl at his recall, but found it hard. She was too replete with the most delicious dinner she'd ever had: *fileto al sagrantino*—meat cooked in a local wine sauce—washed down with a full-bodied red wine. And the most gorgeous man on the planet right across from her.

Lust was winding a delicious tension tighter and tighter inside her. She hoped that Gianni couldn't see the neediness he evoked in her.

Thankfully the waiter interrupted them, taking away plates, asking about dessert. Keelin shook her head. 'I'm too full.'

Gianni ordered coffees and Keelin wanted to shift his focus off her.

'Why did you decide to buy a home here?'

He looked at her. 'It was through my grand-father. When he moved to Rome originally he used to come here to learn more about foods and wines, and then he brought me with him, educating me. Along with the summers in Sicily they were magical trips. He was a good teacher.'

His mouth tightened. 'His own son wasn't interested in what he loved most, but I was. I lapped it up.'

Keelin felt that empathy again. 'And then had to watch as your father threw it all away. That must have been hard.'

Gianni shrugged, expression veiled now. 'I'm just sorry Nonno's not here to see the fruits of his labour taking off again.'

'When did he die?'

'When I was eleven.'

An impressionable age. The same age as Keelin had been when she'd realised she'd have no role to play in her own family business. She said huskily, 'He'd be proud, I'm sure.'

The coffees arrived and Keelin took a quick sip, needing to dilute some of this dreamy ef-fect she was feeling.

'And what about you?' Gianni asked now. 'Apart from wanting to prove yourself to your father, there must have been a moment when you knew that you wanted to be in the business?'

Keelin felt as if he was peeling her skin back

and looking underneath. She reluctantly told him about her fascination with the business ever since she was small. And how she'd artlessly declared her intention to be part of it.

'Unfortunately, my grandfather wasn't like yours. He saw no merit in passing on his learning to a mere granddaughter. But if I'd been a *boy* it would have been totally different.'

She'd never revealed the extent of her ambition to anyone before but it wasn't as if Gianni wasn't aware of how far she'd been prepared to go to fight for her independence. And look how well that had turned out. She was sitting here, dining with the enemy, having let him see her at her most vulnerable and exposed.

For a moment, the extent to which Gianni had got under her skin was suddenly clear and stark. And unwelcome. Assuring herself that she was still in control, she continued, 'I would have happily left school to work for nothing, learning everything from the ground up. I used to sit in on my father's meetings and listen to him, until he put me out.'

'What aspect of it interests you most?'

Keelin's heart thumped and she looked at Gianni suspiciously but he seemed to be genuine. She fiddled with her cup. 'I'm interested in innovation. Going out and researching the market, seeing what other companies are doing and trying to get ahead of the curve. I think that's the key to longevity and success, apart from building on the tried and tested brands.'

Gianni nodded slowly. 'I agree. I think if O'Connor's has one failing it's in this area. Have you ever mentioned it to your father?'

Keelin smiled but it was bitter. 'Lots of times, but he never listened. My grandfather had entrenched views of women's abilities and he passed that down to my father. I was aware of his disappointment in me, always, for not being a son.'

Gianni was surprised at the angry surge of emotion rising within him. He could picture Keelin as a small earnest girl all too easily, her face crestfallen as she was disappointed over and over again.

He heard himself say fiercely, 'I would never stop my daughter from doing what she wanted.'

He wasn't sure who was more surprised by that, himself or Keelin. He hadn't even realised he'd held that opinion until it was out in the open between them.

Keelin's eyes widened. 'Good, because no girl should ever feel that anything is out of her reach.'

Something seemed to stretch between them, an accord. Tenuous and delicate. Gianni's eyes dropped to Keelin's ring finger and he stood up abruptly, putting some money down on the table.

'I want to take you somewhere.'

'Which one do you like?'

This is what Keelin had been afraid of. They were in a jeweller's—one of the many glittering shops open late for the strolling tourists—and several trays of rings were laid out in front of her. Each display more exquisite than the last. And aeons removed from the ostentatious rock he'd presented her with that first week they'd met.

'Gianni,' she said weakly, mindful of the attentive assistant, 'you don't have to do this. I already have a ring.'

'Keelin, we're not leaving until you choose one.'

He was as immovable as a stone wall on the chair beside her. She rolled her eyes and grumbled, 'So bossy.'

The truth was that a ring had jumped out at her from the moment she'd set eyes on it and now she looked at it again. Gianni followed her eyeline and picked the ring out, saying a little incredulously, '*This* one?'

Feeling defensive, she said, 'I know it's not exactly flashy but I like it. It's simple but stunning.'

The shop assistant cleared his throat then

and said a little reproachfully, 'I have to agree
with your wife's impeccable taste, Signor Delucca. This ring is from the art deco period and
is a prime example of its era with the simple
baguette-cut emerald and two smaller diamonds
on either side.'

Gianni took Keelin's hand and before she
could stop him he slid it onto her ring finger to
nestle alongside her wedding band. Her heart
lurched. It looked *right*.

It was almost with relief that she said, 'It's
too big.'

The assistant hurriedly assured them that it
could be resized within days. Keelin took it off
and handed it over, feeling a tumult of emotions
and an awful kind of regret that Gianni wasn't
presenting her with a ring out of *love*. That rogue
thought made her go clammy with fear.

Was it really only hours ago he'd so coldly
given her a choice to walk away?

Suddenly feeling claustrophobic and increasingly panicky, Keelin got up, muttering something about needing air, and stepped out of the
shop, leaving Gianni to deal with the payment.

Love? Since when had that been part of the
equation? She spied a small shop across the
street and ducked in to get some water, gulping
it gratefully. It was the lingering heat from the

day. Heat did funny things to your brain. Like give you delusions.

Gianni appeared outside the jeweller's shop looking left and right. Clearly he couldn't see her in the shadows across the street. As she watched he frowned impatiently and something in her eased slightly to see that familiar impatience.

She wasn't in love with him. She wanted him. So he'd bought her a ring? It wasn't as if he'd pretended it was for any other reason than because she wouldn't wear the other one.

She stepped out of her hiding place and Gianni's gaze settled on her immediately. He relaxed visibly and suddenly Keelin didn't feel so sanguine. He closed the distance between them and captured her close. More heat exploded, so much that she thought she might faint from it.

'What now?' she asked as airily as she could, as if she hadn't just had a mild panic attack at the thought that she might be falling in love with this man.

Gianni's gaze had dropped to her mouth. He bent his head and his tongue darted out to lick some stray drops of water. Keelin shuddered, arousal spiking in her blood.

He pulled back and saw it, and it was mirrored in his eyes. He growled softly, 'There's only one place I want to be right now, and it's not in a public street.'

* * *

Much later that night Keelin lay draped across Gianni's chest and his hand was moving idly up and down her bare back. The sweat was still cooling on their spent bodies.

Keelin was feeling a sense of bliss that was dangerous because the cause of it was the mass of hard hewn muscle under her cheek. She knew he was still awake too, because she could feel a relaxed tension in his body.

She'd been dying to ask him a question and now felt that with the darkness cloaking them that maybe she could.

She lifted her head a little. 'Gianni?'

A half-grunting sound of acknowledgement came. 'Hmm?'

Keelin half whispered, half spoke. 'Why didn't you end up in the Mafia like your father? How did you avoid it?'

The sleepy tension left his body, every muscle locked hard now. Keelin immediately said, 'It's okay, I shouldn't have asked.'

For a long time Gianni said nothing and she thought she'd seriously overstepped the mark, but just when she was thinking he wouldn't answer, his chest rumbled and he said, 'I never got involved because I saw what it did to my mother, who lived in constant fear, and my grandfather.

He stood up to my father's henchmen once and they beat him for it. My father did nothing.'

Keelin lifted her head again. 'Gianni...'

'I didn't see it as remotely glamorous or exciting. But the fact is that when I think about it now, my father never let me come near any of his activities. Not that I wanted to, but it was almost as if he deliberately kept me with my grandfather more than him, and after Nonno died, he seemed to go out of his way to antagonise me, make me despise him.'

Keelin said quietly, 'Maybe he did it on purpose to force you not to follow in his footsteps. Maybe he was trapped somehow.'

Gianni didn't answer. Keelin's heart tugged at the thought of a teenage Gianni, so proud and righteous, protecting his mother, vowing to be nothing like his father.

He spoke again. 'Sometimes I'm afraid that I have his violence inside me and some day it'll come out and I won't be able to control it, in spite of trying to get as far away from it as I can.'

Now Keelin tensed, everything in her rejecting his words. She moved up so that she was chest to chest with Gianni, and said with a surprising level of fierceness, 'You wouldn't hurt a fly.'

She could see the cynical gleam of his smile in the dark. 'You barely know me.'

She still felt fierce. 'I know you enough. And you wouldn't hurt anyone. Violence isn't wired into your DNA. You grew up with it, that's all, so you're more aware of it.'

Gianni moved then, suddenly, displaying his superior strength as he flipped Keelin so that he loomed over her in the dark. She wrapped her arms around his neck, feeling an inordinate amount of emotion for this man.

'You don't scare me.'

Gianni shook his head, negating what Keelin said—what the hell did she know of the darkness he sometimes experienced?—but something inside him felt inexplicably lightened.

It was only just now that he'd had that realisation that his father had always, *always*, made sure that Gianni was nowhere near any of his endeavours. Even though it was traditional for the Mafia guys to groom their sons to follow in their footsteps.

Feeling ridiculously vulnerable for the first time in a long time, when Keelin brought her mouth up to touch his, he fell on her like a starving man, and the uncomfortable revelations faded to the back of his mind, for now. And the fact that Keelin had soothed a part of him that he'd never shared with anyone else.

* * *

The end of the week of the honeymoon came
and went and Gianni had still made no move to
go back to Rome, even though he felt the need
to do so like an annoying burr under his skin.
But the fact was that the lure to stay and indulge
himself making love to his wife was far more
powerful.

He'd looked at the woman—exhausted—in
the bed beside him that morning and cursed her
roundly. *Merda.*

He'd taken this week out to focus on his new
wife and give her some sense of security in the
marriage and get to know her. But the worry-
ing thing was that he couldn't seem to envisage
a time when he would feel relaxed enough to
leave Keelin to her own devices so that he could
get back to work.

It was almost as if, superstitiously, he knew
that leaving this place would break something
apart that felt very fragile. And would also remind him of things that he was deliberately
pushing to the back of his mind, like since when
had he ever had the compulsion to indulge in a
domestic idyll?

Staff had returned to the villa from their
week's holiday and the place resumed its usual
busy efficiency. Gianni had distracted himself
when he wasn't with Keelin with half-hearted

attempts to focus on things that needed to be attended to there.

Like his plans for a new vineyard and newer plans to open a stables. He'd just spoken to his friend Gio Corretti in Sicily, who he'd rung for advice on the matter, and something about hearing Gio's children laughing and playing in the background had made something inside Gianni ache a little. Something completely alien and new.

He hadn't told Keelin about those plans and he didn't like how his decision made him feel a little exposed. He told himself it had nothing to do with the fact that she loved horses and that he'd thought about it after bringing her to a local stables the other day, where they'd spent the day on horseback. Her pure undiluted joy had been infectious and he'd practically had to drag her away, she'd been so happily mucking in. He also told himself it had nothing to do with the fact that he'd seen her smile, *like that*. Exactly like the photo in her father's office.

It was a clinical decision based on the fact that he was merely trying to do everything he could to make Keelin feel as at home as possible.

He frowned now—where was she anyway? He got up and left his study and found her in the small garden outside the kitchen, planting herbs with Lucia. Their backs were to him so he could watch them for a minute.

Keelin rested back on her heels, wiping her brow. She was frowning and saying in halting Italian, *'Buondìa, buongiorno, buonanotte...'*

Lucia was beaming and saying, *'Bene, molto bene.'*

Keelin smiled. *'Grazie mille.'*

Gianni felt his chest get tight to hear Lucia conducting a rudimentary Italian lesson. The earth under his feet was moving, shifting. As if sensing him, Keelin looked around and smiled.

Dammit. The tight feeling increased.

She rose to her feet with a lithe move, displaying her long bare legs in cut-off shorts and her stunning curves in a halterneck top. A straw hat protected her delicate pale skin from the sun; even so, she was acquiring freckles and a golden glow.

Gianni had the most bizarre desire to never leave this place, and to feel her arms slide around him so that he could rest his head on her breast and experience a measure of peace and security that had eluded him all of his life.

She stopped before him and tilted her head. 'Why are you looking at me like that?'

Before that incisive green gaze might see too much, Gianni grabbed her hand and all but dragged her into the villa. By the time they were in the bedroom with the door shut firmly behind them, they were mutually ravenous—tearing at clothes and falling into the bed in a tangle of limbs, mouths meeting with a clash of tongue and teeth.

Gianni weakly welcomed the equilibrium he regained as he embedded himself deep in Keelin's slick heat. All he wanted right now were these incandescent moments that drowned out the voices screaming, *What the hell is going on here?*

Early the following morning as dawn rose, Gianni left a sleeping Keelin in bed. He couldn't seem to rest, even though his body was sated in a way that made him nervous. Sated, but still ravenous. As if he was being kept on a knife edge at all times. It was disconcerting.

In his study he noted the flashing lights of about a million messages and passed his hand over his face wearily. Before he listened to them he opened the top drawer of his desk and pulled out the small velvet box that had been delivered the previous day.

Opening it, the emerald ring Keelin had chosen in the shop in Montefalco glittered up at him. It seemed to mock him for lots of things. For being so careless with his first choice of ring. For believing her ridiculous charade at the start. For not realising that despite her natural unfussiness, she had an innate style and grace.

He hadn't given it to her yet. Something was holding him back and he hated that it wasn't just something he could do without feeling as if suddenly some kind of meaning was attached.

Gianni sighed and closed the box, putting it back in the drawer. And then he picked up the phone to listen to his messages. As he listened to message after message, his world stopped turning and his previous thoughts and feelings reverberated in his head, mocking him loudly.

He finally put down the phone. Shock made him feel sluggish. And all he could think about and *feel* was the incredible sting of betrayal. And think of the woman in the bed upstairs, the woman who had given him her innocence in a bid to make him believe that she was innocent through and through. When she wasn't at all.

One of the most important lessons his father had ever taught him—inadvertently—was that you could only trust yourself. In the Mafia, where the code was loyalty and family, everyone knew that at any moment your own brother could shoot you in the back, so that stuff about family and loyalty? It was all rubbish.

Ever since Gianni had looked at that photograph of Keelin on the horse, and seen something pure in her smiling face—something he'd believed didn't exist—he'd been behaving like a fool. And now he stood to lose everything.

The fact that she had to be guilty was unequivocal. She'd played him from the start and he'd fallen for it. She'd gone to incredible lengths to distract him, and ultimately seduce him so that he didn't realise what was going on. Hadn't she admitted to him that she'd do anything to prove her loyalty to her father? Well, she just had, by running so many rings around him that he didn't know if he was coming or going.

He made a call, an awful terrifying feeling of rage spreading to every limb, turning him icy. Icy was better. He'd been too consumed with heat, and look where that had left him—in serious jeopardy.

He spoke into the phone, his voice curt. 'Have the helicopter ready within half an hour and tell them I'm on my way.'

When Keelin woke she had a strange sense of déjà vu. And then a sound broke into her consciousness. She cracked open her eyes and noted that she was spreadeagled across the bed, gloriously naked.

A tumble of images came into her head, of Gianni dragging her up to the room yesterday, and of how he'd been remorseless...in his determination to send her over the edge. So many times that she'd been begging for mercy.

They'd finally fallen asleep and the sound made Keelin frown. It was louder now. A rhythmic *thwack thwack*.

The helicopter. She went cold. *No*. Gianni would not have done this again.

She got out of bed and scrabbled for clothes, dragging on her shorts and a T-shirt. She raced downstairs and to the front of the villa, opening the door just in time to see the helicopter rise into the air from the back of the villa.

There were two figures in the seats, and one was unmistakably her husband. For a moment Keelin felt a lurch of panic—perhaps something had happened?

But Gianni made no attempt to look down, his gaze firmly set on the distance where they were headed. The machine banked left and then it took off over the estate and towards the horizon.

And he was gone. Just like before. Without even saying goodbye. Except this time there was no reason—she hadn't made him angry.

Frowning, and not liking the slightly sick sensation in her belly, Keelin went back inside and looked in Gianni's study to see if he'd left a note. But there was nothing.

Then she thought she might have missed

something in the bedroom, but again there was
nothing.

She could hear movement and realised that
this wasn't as bad as the last time. Now she
knew that people were around, and also, she had
the somewhat unsettling realisation that even if
others weren't around, she wouldn't have that
awful sense of abandonment.

But the hours crept by and there was no sign
or call from Gianni to explain where he'd gone.
And any kind of confidence Keelin had been
feeling started to crumble, like blocks that
weren't steady enough yet to weather any undue
force.

She smiled as Lucia served her lunch, valiantly trying out the few words she'd been learning. And now she felt silly. What had she been
doing for the past few days? Fooling herself
into believing that somehow everything began
and ended with this villa? That the real world
wouldn't encroach and remind her that this was
all just a mirage?

She'd had the strong suspicion that Gianni
had just gone out of his way to seduce her into
believing that she might be happy as his wife.

And by the time evening rolled around with
still no sign of her husband, Keelin was coming
to terms with the fact that clearly he felt that he'd
spent enough time lulling his wife into a false

sense of security so why would he need to hang around for longer than necessary?

All day and evening, Keelin had resisted the urge to call Gianni, believing the onus was on him to explain himself. And now she seethed and hated the familiar sense of powerlessness and that she was being ignored.

But she was no longer helpless.

Before Lucia disappeared to bed, Keelin found her and managed to find out what time the train to Rome was in the morning.

There was no way that Gianni was going to get away with believing that she would be happy to sit quietly at his rural home and await his return. She was so focused on her anger that when she took a stingingly hot shower and emotion rose up in a wave it shocked her.

Sob after heaving sob erupted from her chest, tears coursing down her cheeks to merge with the hot water. Aghast at this outpouring but unable to stop it, Keelin shut off the shower and stepped out, her chest still heaving slightly.

Feeling shell-shocked, she looked at her face in the mirror and saw puffy swollen eyes. And she had to finally acknowledge the truth that she'd been resisting all day, and since Montefalco, if she was honest.

The worst thing had happened. She'd fallen in love with her husband. She'd fallen in love with a man who would never love her back. His actions today only proved that.

After all she'd been through, she'd learnt nothing, except that the defences she'd so carefully erected long ago had started tumbling as soon as she'd locked onto that black gaze.

And all the while Gianni had just been playing with her. Proving his dominance. Ruthlessly dismissing her own wishes and desires in a bid to get what he wanted. His cynicism knew no bounds. For the past week he'd wooed her with his body and attention, only to drop her from a height.

And now Keelin looked at herself and felt despair at her lovelorn expression. Was she really so pathetic? So she'd fallen in love with a man who had never made any promises to do the same. If anything, he'd been nothing but brutally honest with her. So she had no one to blame but herself.

But she knew what she had to do. It was time to end this charade once and for all—deal or no deal. And if that meant sacrificing her deepest desires, then she would do it and move on. Because nothing was worth a lifetime of unrequited love. She'd already been defined by that and she wouldn't allow it to define her again.

CHAPTER TEN

WHEN KEELIN GOT off the train in Rome she was hot and sweaty. And angry. She buried all of her vulnerabilities under the fire in her belly. No way would Gianni ever know how much he'd hurt her.

She hailed a taxi and gave them directions for Gianni's offices and apartment building. When they arrived she made her way to the private lift. The doorman, Lorenzo, recognised her and said, 'Signora Delucca, shall I inform your husband you're on your way up?'

Keelin pushed down the flutter of nerves. 'Is he in his office?'

The man nodded. 'I believe so.'

Keelin forced a smile. 'Then yes, that would be great.'

The lift doors opened and she went in, relishing the air conditioning. As the elevator ascended silently though, her palms got sweaty with nerves.

The lift stopped and the doors opened to reveal Gianni with his hands on his hips and a hard expression on his face. 'What are you doing here?'

Keelin was so taken aback for a moment that she could only open her mouth. He was angry. Blisteringly angry. *Why?* She was the one who should be angry. If anything it made things easier to see the depth of his displeasure that she'd climbed out of the box he'd put her in.

'I thought I told you never to leave me like that again.'

Gianni sneered. 'Spare me a repeat of the sob story, Keelin. I don't have time for this.'

Keelin's gasp of outrage was almost swallowed up by the doors starting to close again and she pushed the button to keep them open.

'*What* did you just say?'

Gianni was icy. 'You heard me. I have no desire to talk to you right now. Go back to Umbria, or go to hell, I don't really care. But don't for a second assume that I'm not going to deal with you.'

Gianni stepped back and turned to walk away. The lift doors started closing again and Keelin stepped out, uncomfortably aware of her jeans and sleeveless loose top, a light jumper tied around her waist.

She followed him in shock at his words. 'What

the hell is that supposed to mean? I'm not the one who took off in a helicopter at the crack of dawn to avoid saying goodbye.'

Gianni whirled around and Keelin noticed for the first time that he hadn't shaved and his clothes were creased.

'Damn you, O'Connor. If you want to do this now, *fine.*'

He took her arm in a punishing grip and ignored her gasp of surprise, all but frog-marching her into his office and slamming the door shut.

Keelin was reeling. *Damn you, O'Connor?* Did he really hate that she'd followed him here that much?

He let her go and strode to his desk, turning around before it and crossing his arms. 'Well,' he asked eventually, 'how much did you know?'

Keelin felt increasingly like Alice in Wonderland. 'Know what?'

Gianni laughed but it was curt and harsh. When he stopped he said, 'I wondered what you'd go for—either denial or petulance.'

She shook her head. 'I have no idea what you're talking about.'

Gianni turned around to his desk and picked up a newspaper. He threw it across the room where it landed at Keelin's feet, face up. As she bent down to pick it up, a headline registered slowly onto her sluggish brain: O'Connor Foods Goes into Receivership.

Keelin scanned the piece and certain words jumped out: *On the cards for months... Last-ditch efforts to save itself by merging with other companies... Will its newest star association, Delucca Emporium, survive this fall? Unlikely.*

Comprehension sank in. She recalled her father turning so pale on the wedding day when Gianni had been late. No wonder. She looked up and Gianni was more remote than she'd ever seen him. Eyes like black holes that looked like they wanted to incinerate her on the spot.

Faintly she said, 'That's why you left so suddenly.'

He clapped slowly. '*Brava.* Your keen understanding of the nuances of this news is truly astonishing.'

Keelin was too shocked for his sarcasm to really penetrate.

Her hand tightened around the paper. 'I didn't know anything about this. You can't possibly think I did, do you?'

But that was a rhetorical question.

Gianni pretended to consider for a moment and then said musingly, 'Let me see, from the moment we've met, you've displayed a dizzying array of roles in an obvious effort to distract me from what your real agenda was.'

Keelin opened her mouth to defend herself again but he cut her off brutally. 'Don't bother wasting your breath. The answer is yes, I absolutely believe you were all over this. Your father has admitted that your role was crucial—via the marriage of convenience, so that when he went down, I'd feel somehow obliged to step in and save him, for the sake of family ties. The depth of your collusion with him is astonishing. He knew he was in trouble and your loyalty knew no bounds, even going so far as to fake disharmony.'

Keelin gasped at that injustice. 'I did not collude with my father, anything but. Everything I told you was true—I *didn't* want to marry you. I just went along with it to placate him.'

The extent of her father's machinations was too horrific to absorb under Gianni's disgusted gaze and he saved her the need to do so. He put up a hand. 'Save it. I'm done. We're done, Keelin. That divorce you wanted so badly? It's yours. Now get out. I never want to see you again.'

Gianni felt nothing as he watched Keelin flounder, her skin as pale as alabaster, the golden lustre of the last week leached away. He felt nothing because ice flowed through his veins.

A voice urged him that perhaps he was being

too hasty? But he shut it down. From day one Keelin had been running rings around him. Doing her best to distract him with enough smoke and mirrors to make sure he didn't look too closely at the deal, or suspect that O'Connor was in trouble.

The longer Keelin stood there though, the more he could feel the ice thawing in his veins, being replaced by heat. He curled his hands around his desk behind him and gripped it so tight he heard his knuckles crack.

Damn her. Why wasn't she moving? He felt something surge inside him, something terrible and wild. Uncontrollable. 'Get out, Keelin.'

She seemed to come out of some sort of shocked trance and she looked as if she might say something, and without even knowing what he was doing, Gianni found himself standing in front of her feeling nothing but pure rage. He told himself that it stemmed from having been betrayed professionally, but he knew that it stemmed from a much more personal betrayal.

If possible she went even paler. But then she stepped up to him and said very deliberately, 'I told you that you don't scare me. You're not your father, Gianni.'

She turned then and left, and Gianni caught sight of his reflection in a mirror. For a moment he almost didn't recognise his own twisted features. He looked at his hands and noticed that they were shaking.

Why had she just done that? Said that? Had she seen it on his face? And known that he might see himself and think the worst?

Damn her. She knew too much, that was all, and right to the last was trying to distract him with smoke and mirrors.

Three weeks later

'Signor Delucca can't be disturbed.'

Keelin tried to maintain a calm facade in the face of the frosty reception she was receiving from Gianni's staff. She hadn't got as far as the lift today before someone had stopped her. She had no doubt that her husband had left very clear instructions where she was concerned. Namely, not to admit her under any circumstances.

It didn't go unnoticed that Lorenzo, the doorman, was gone. Had he been fired for letting her into the inner sanctum? Somehow when Keelin thought of Gianni on that last day, she wouldn't doubt it.

'I'll wait.'

The sleek efficient-looking brunette was disapproving. 'Miss O'Connor, I really can't recommend—'

Keelin felt irritation rise. 'It's still Signora De-lucca, and I said I'll wait. *Grazie.*'

She went and sat down in one of the plush chairs near the receptionist's desk, staring straight ahead, her hands on her leather brief-case. She felt hot and prickly at the thought of seeing Gianni again, but determined.

She'd arrived in Rome from Dublin a short time before, dressed as if she was going to an interview in a sober dark grey trouser suit and court shoes, hair tamed into a chignon.

Keelin heard the woman on the phone, pre-sumably to Gianni, speaking in low hushed tones and too fast for her to make out any words. But of course there was no sign of him.

To her chagrin, she couldn't get moments of their time together out of her head, like a bad movie running on a loop. And as time ticked on, Keelin became more and more determined, anger at Gianni festering like a ball of acid in her belly. She could absolutely understand why he was so livid with her but there was no evidence to support his accusations of her involvement. It merely proved how duped she'd become— believing that something had changed between them in Umbria.

He'd played her like a virtuoso—especially with that whole letting her go so that she'd come back act. He'd known her better than she had herself. Damn him. But he would never guess how she felt. She'd come today because, in spite of everything, she owed him. Her father owed him, but he was too much of a mess to sort anything out.

She would do what she'd come to do and then go back to Dublin and pick up the pieces of her life. A life where her family business no longer existed. To her surprise, all she'd been feeling in relation to that news had been a sense of liberation.

The receptionist was packing up her stuff for the day and Keelin looked at her watch in despair. But just then the phone rang and the girl picked it up. She looked at Keelin and then appeared to pout slightly before replying and hanging up.

She came over to Keelin and said, 'You may go up to Signor Delucca's office. He will see you now.'

Keelin stood up and made her way to the lift, muscles stiff after sitting for so long. When the elevator doors opened to admit her to his floor she held her breath in case he was on the other side again, breathing fire.

But the space was empty. Keelin stepped out and approached his door when it swung open suddenly, and he was filling it. She just about held in a gasp. He was seriously dishevelled and his jaw was dark with the growth of a beard. Hadn't he shaved since she'd seen him? And did he look tired or was that just her imagination?

'You're not going to leave, are you?'

She shook her head. 'Five minutes, Gianni, that's all I ask. Please.'

For a long moment he just stood there and then he stepped back, indicating silently for her to come into his office. He didn't move out of the way completely, so when she walked through, her body brushed against his and she had to repress a shudder of longing.

He closed the door and she turned to face him. His face definitely looked more lined and Keelin felt a pang and immediately quashed it, putting it down to business concerns and nothing more personal.

She hated that *she* looked so obviously wan and tired. She couldn't bear to be under his disdainful scrutiny for longer than necessary so she said in a rush, 'I've just come to show—' She stopped and amended, 'Well, to give you something.'

Gianni moved into the office to come and stand behind his desk, arms crossed. Keelin had been keeping up with business news and had been relieved to see that while her father going into receivership had undoubtedly hurt Gianni, it looked as though it was mainly a PR disaster and not necessarily a financial one.

She'd winced to see the rumours abound about why he'd got involved with O'Connor in the first place. And the resurgence of all the old speculation about links to the Mafia.

Keelin put her briefcase on a chair and opened it up, taking out a sheaf of papers. When she looked up Gianni was completely impassive. She steeled herself and put the papers on his desk and drew herself up tall, eyeballing him bravely.

'This is a contract, signed by me.'

'Divorce papers?' he asked hopefully, and then, 'You really didn't have to come here personally.'

Keelin swallowed the flash of irritation. 'No, I'll be signing those next week once my solicitor has changed them so that I receive nothing from you.'

His brows snapped together. 'What—'

She put up a hand. 'That's not why I'm here anyway. I'm signing over almost sixty per cent worth of shares in O'Connor's to you. It's enough to try and negotiate with the receivers to let you take control and build it up again, should you so wish.'

Keelin answered his unspoken question. 'You're probably wondering how I got the shares?'

He nodded, giving nothing away. She took a breath. 'I started buying them up as soon as I knew what had happened, with my savings. And I persuaded my mother to sign her shares over to me. She's never had any interest anyway and my father isn't capable of much at the moment. All of his board have lost confidence in him. They'll never accept him as CEO again.'I've also given you a complete set of the most recent accounts and all of our contacts for clients.'

Gianni was stony. 'Why are you doing this, Keelin?'

She forced herself to endure that black gaze a little longer. 'I'm doing it because you didn't deserve to be brought down with my father. He was dishonest about the extent of O'Connor's problems. And I know if anyone can turn it around again, it's you.'

She fought not to show any emotion and unconsciously hitched up her chin. 'I've realised that my obsession with wanting to be a part of the business really stemmed from wanting my father's attention. He loved the business and I believed that if I could be part of it he'd love me too.'

She smiled but it was brittle. 'It's pathetic, I know. And it's not that I'm not interested any more but I know I'm not qualified to take this on, on my own.

'You're welcome to it, Gianni. And for what it's worth, I truly didn't know what was going on. I'm sorry, you didn't deserve this, but neither did I. I was as much of a pawn in my father's machinations as you were.'

And then she took off her wedding ring and put it on the table, on top of the papers.

She picked up her briefcase and walked quickly to the door, her throat tight. She reached for the door handle but found that she couldn't just turn it and walk out. An unstoppable urge was rising within her and it galvanised her to turn around again.

She blurted out, 'I know this marriage was only ever a business contract to you, but it became something else for me when we were in Umbria. I know that you were just trying to make me believe a marriage could work but for a short time I thought it might. I was wrong. In any case, you helped me see that I can be strong enough to withstand the worst thing of all, and it wasn't what I always imagined it would be, losing my inheritance for good.'

Keelin turned again and found the doorknob and turned it, pulling the door open. She heard nothing from behind her, not a word to stop or wait. So she swallowed her grief and kept walking, into the lift, down to the lobby and out of Gianni's building and out of his life, for good.

* * *

Gianni looked at the closed door for a long moment. Had he just dreamed it? Keelin walking in? Giving him the papers, effectively signing over her family business? The business she'd entered into a sham marriage for?

He looked down and saw the sheaf of papers and the wedding ring on top. It had happened. That uniquely floral scent on the air wasn't a mirage. Mocking him like the torrid dreams he was having whenever he closed his eyes for more than five minutes.

He sank down into his seat, feeling as if someone had just punched him in the belly. Her words came back to him as if through a fog: *I know this marriage was only ever a business contract to you, but it became something else for me when we were in Umbria.*

For the past three weeks Gianni had been hauled over the coals and roasted alive by his peers and clients and future clients. A dozen deals had fallen through. People looked and whispered in public. People mentioned *Mafia*, and sins of the fathers. Even his mother had been concerned enough to come to visit him. It was his worst nightmare come to life. But did he care a whit about that?

No.

He'd been consumed by something else. And

that something else was five foot eight with red hair and curves that had looked dramatically *less* just now. And she was walking away from him because she believed he never wanted to see her again.

And he'd told himself he hadn't. But it wasn't the truth. Because suddenly everything was crystal clear and Gianni found himself taking his first proper breath in weeks. And it was so heady that it hurt.

Galvanised far too late, he left his office and went down to the street, heart banging against his chest. But of course she was gone.

'Lamb for table one, ready to go.'

'I've got it,' Keelin said, shoving her order book back into the pocket at the front of her apron and stabbing the pen into the bun on the top of her head. She reached for the plate and deftly balanced it with another one for the same table.

When she was walking back to the hatch area she rolled her neck tiredly. Every muscle was screaming with fatigue but she welcomed it because it kept her brain numb and she needed to feel numb. Because if the numbness went, then she'd fall apart.

The manager called her over and handed her a menu, 'A guy just sat down on table three without waiting to be seated. If we weren't having a slow night I'd say something but he's so gorgeous that we'll forgive him.'

Keelin smiled at her old college friend who had happened to be looking for waiters for her new business when Keelin had bumped into her two days ago when she'd arrived back from Rome.

'Leave it with me. I'll try not to scare him off.'

Keelin walked over, taking the menu with her, her mouth open and ready to list off the specials for the evening, when she stopped in her tracks and her mouth stayed open.

Gianni Delucca was sitting at the table, dominating the space around him and standing out effortlessly in the small hipster Temple Bar eaterie. For a second she felt so light-headed she thought she might faint. But Gianni must have seen something on her face and was half standing as if to help her.

She rushed over, grating through the waves of shock, 'What are you doing here?'

He sat back down looking entirely unrepentant. 'Looking for you.' Now he was grating, 'Why the hell didn't you let your solicitor know where you're staying?'

Keelin flushed. 'Because I'm in a hostel until I can afford somewhere of my own.'

If Gianni had come to crow, then now would

be a really good time. Keelin was hot, sweaty and making a pittance an hour and living in a hostel. He should feel that justice had been served.

'We need to talk.'

Keelin blinked. She noted that he looked more like himself than he had the last time she'd seen him. His hair was neat again, he was clean-shaven. Even if he still had a more lean look than usual.

Angry that she was noticing him, when evidently Gianni wanted to punish her some more, she snapped, 'Well, I can't just leave. My shift doesn't end for at least two hours.'

She turned to go, taking the menus with her, but Gianni caught her arm, and the seismic reaction to his touch in her body made her stop. She turned back. 'Let me *go.*'

'No. Not unless you agree to come with me. Now.'

Keelin opened her mouth to argue but something in his eyes stopped her. She recognised that steely look too well.

'Fine, I'll ask. But if she can't let me go, then you'll just have to wait.'

He finally released her arm and Keelin had to fight the urge to rub where he'd touched her as if he'd burnt her skin. Damn him.

She went back over to Susan and explained

the situation reluctantly. Her friend's eyes widened. 'He's your husband?'

'Soon to be *ex*,' Keelin said hastily, thinking of the divorce papers she'd signed just yesterday.

Her friend said dreamily, 'Somehow I don't think you'll be coming back for more shifts, but it's okay. I totally forgive you.'

Keelin rolled her eyes and hated that her heart lurched at that. Gianni was here to talk to her about O'Connor's, no doubt. She took off her apron and got her bag from under the counter and went straight out the door, not even bothering to see if he was following her.

He caught up with her easily and said, 'We'll go to my hotel, it's private.'

Keelin stopped and looked at him. She was very conscious of being in her waitress's outfit of a black skirt and white shirt, smelling distinctly of *eau de kitchen*.

And it was seriously disconcerting to see Gianni in Dublin against the dusky sky. 'Where are you staying?'

He named a hotel which was naturally the most exclusive and expensive in Dublin, and suddenly Keelin had a vision of them in a sumptuous private space and she balked at the thought.

She shook her head and said firmly, 'No,

there's a coffee shop in my hostel, and it's closer. We'll go there.'

Gianni's mouth tightened but he said nothing and then eventually, 'Fine, lead the way.'

Ten minutes later they were entering a very rustic and hippyesque lobby of one of Dublin's busiest hostels. Keelin went into the coffee shop part of it and asked for two coffees, acutely aware that all the tourist backpackers were blinking at this glorious specimen of masculinity in their midst.

She almost regretted coming here, but then had to admit to some sense of satisfaction when she saw Gianni lower himself gingerly onto a very threadbare-looking chair beside hers.

She wrapped her hands around her coffee and cut to the chase. 'Why are you here?'

Gianni responded a little incredulously, 'You really want to do this here?'

Keelin nodded, now more than ever, because the more it sank in that he was here, the more she wanted to reach out and touch him.

Gianni shrugged minutely under his pristine jacket and took a sip of coffee before putting it down. He speared her with that black gaze. 'I owe you an apology.'

Keelin went still. 'You do?'

He nodded, looking serious. 'I automatically assumed you were in on the downfall of

O'Connor's and I shouldn't have. You gave me no reason to believe that you would collude with your father, anything but.'

Something deflated inside Keelin. 'You spoke to my father? Or you figured it out because I'm not mentioned anywhere?'

Gianni shook his head. 'No, I didn't check anything. I didn't need to. Once I could see clearly again I knew the truth but I jumped to the worst conclusion because it was easier than dealing with my emotions.'

Keelin felt a little dizzy even though she was sitting down. She frowned. 'Emotions, what do you mean?'

Gianni sighed and ran a hand through his hair, a sign of his inner agitation. He looked at her. 'I need to know what you meant just before you left that last day when you said that the marriage had become something else and what you meant about losing O'Connor's not being the worst thing.'

Keelin said faintly, 'It's not enough that I gave you everything?'

Gianni shook his head, resolute. 'I need to know.'

Anger surged inside Keelin to think that he was going to take her feelings and use them to torture her. She put down her coffee, and clenched her hands, saying fiercely, 'Damn you, Gianni Delucca. I wish I'd never set eyes on you. Everything was so much clearer before you came along. I knew who I was and what I wanted.'

He looked pained. 'Do you really mean that?'

Keelin shook her head and nodded at the same time, anger draining away. 'No. Yes. *No.*'

And then Gianni shocked her by moving onto his knees before her, right there in the lobby of the hostel. Keelin darted a look around, aware of the avid interest. 'What are you doing?'

He ignored her question and asked again, 'What did you mean?'

Keelin felt shaky. The way Gianni was looking at her, she'd never seen him like this before, stripped of all artifice and arrogance. He looked younger, vulnerable. And she thought about his father, and grandfather, and how important it was to him to fix the past, and her heart swelled.

She finally admitted huskily, 'When I stopped fighting you and fighting being married to you, I discovered that I liked it. And that I didn't want to keep thinking about ways to get out of it. Losing O'Connor's wasn't the worst thing because losing you was far worse. My whole life was spent seeking a way into my father's affections, or gaining his approval. Then when I knew that would never happen, I transferred it to gaining a place in O'Connor's, but deep down I wanted a soul-deep connection with someone, and when I felt it for you I pushed it away because I was afraid that I was just blindly seeking approval or acceptance all over again.'

Keelin forced herself to be strong. 'So if you've just come here to—'

'I love you.'

Keelin's mouth was still open. 'You *what*?'

The pained look was leaving Gianni's face. 'I love you, Keelin O'Connor. I fell in love with you the day I saw the photo of you in your father's office.'

He went on. 'What you described in Umbria, it was exactly the same for me. So when I heard the news that your father's business had been falling apart for months, I used blaming you as an excuse to avoid admitting that I was falling for you.'

He shook his head. 'I'm so sorry.'

Keelin was in shock. Her brain wasn't processing properly. 'Did you just say that you love me?'

He nodded. 'You've shown me how blinkered I'd become. I was so obsessed with ridding my family of the Delucca Mafia heritage and restoring my grandfather's good name, and then you left and I realised that it's all for nothing without you. I couldn't care less what happens to me or what people say as long as you're with me. I always used my grandfather as inspiration when I needed to be spurred on to succeed, but he loved the simple things, and appreciated love and family above everything, in spite of his son.

'He was so in love with my grandmother that when she died young, he had to leave Sicily because he couldn't bear to be where she wasn't. That's why they moved to Rome, not because he was so ambitious. And I'd forgotten about that. I'd blocked that out, because after seeing my father and mother, I didn't think it existed.'

Keelin's throat was tight with repressed emotion.

'There's something else you should know. As of today my company has a new name.'

'It does?' She almost couldn't get the words past the lump in her throat and chest.

Gianni nodded. 'It's called Delucca & O'Connor Limited. I hope you approve, because you're on the board of directors and we took the vote without you.'

Tears filled Keelin's eyes and she blinked them back furiously. 'Are you sure that—'

He put a finger to her mouth, stopping her words, and said softly, 'I've never been more sure of anything in my life. But there's something else I need to do.'

He pulled a velvet box out of the inside pocket of his jacket and opened it. In the white satin folds nestled the emerald ring from the shop in Montefalco. Keelin had forgotten about it and her eyes widened to see it now, glittering brilliantly.

Gianni took it out of the box and said with a touch of nervousness that made her melt inside, 'I know we're doing this all wrong, but I'd like to ask you something.'

Euphoria was starting to snake through Keelin's blood and hitting her heart, making it pound unevenly. 'What?'

His gaze was intense, burning. 'Keelin O'Connor, would you please consider not going through with the divorce and continuing to be my wife?'

Time felt as if it was suspended. She looked at him for a long moment and saw only the purest form of love in his dark gaze. And even better, love that was requited. With no conditions attached.

She nodded. 'Yes.'

He smiled and took her hand, sliding the ring onto her finger, and then he reached into his pocket again and took out another ring, her wedding band, and tears stung her eyes.

He looked at her as he put it on to join her new engagement ring, saying huskily, 'With this ring I thee re-wed, Keelin O'Connor Delucca.'

She took her hand from his and leaned forward, lacing them behind his neck. She half laughed and smiled, feeling giddy. 'I now pronounce us man and wife. You may kiss the bride.'

Gianni spread her legs with his hands and came between them as much as her skirt would allow and then, pressing her back into the seat, he wrapped both arms around his wife and kissed her so thoroughly that only a persistent clearing of a throat finally brought them up for air.

Keelin was dizzy. Heart pounding. Euphoric.

'Em, excuse me? If you wouldn't mind, this is a public place and you're making the other guests uncomfortable.'

Gianni drew back and Keelin blushed to the roots of her hair when she saw the array of faces staring at them. They looked anything but embarrassed. One couple had even started kissing passionately in another corner and Keelin had to fight back a giggle, feeling truly light for the first time in her life.

Gianni stood up and took her hands, pulling her up. He looked at her mock sternly. 'I am *not* taking you to bed in a hostel.'

Keelin shook her head and just said with emotion high in her voice, 'Take me home, Gianni.'

And hand in hand, he did.

EPILOGUE

'PAPA!'

Gianni smiled at the ecstatic screech that came from a blur of sturdy legs and chubby arms and dark red hair as his two-year-old son launched himself into his outstretched arms and gave him a loud lip-smacking kiss.

'Ciao, piccolino, come stai?'

Piero, named after Gianni's grandfather, proceeded to fill him in on everything in a babble of English and Italian and other incomprehensible words, his dark eyes wide with the urgency to tell his beloved papa everything.

Gianni smiled a greeting at the staff in the créche that had been installed in the ground floor area of his office building in Rome, and he walked out with Piero held high in his arms.

He'd only been in Dublin for the day but even that felt like too long away from his family.

He got into his private lift and said when

he could get a word in edgeways, 'Let's find Mamma, hmm?'

Piero clapped his hands together. *'Mamma e bambino!'*

'Sì.' Gianni kissed his son again, his heart swelling with love and contentment to be back near his family. His mother had finally agreed to sell the family home and now she divided her time between the apartment in Rome and the villa in Umbria and had become a new woman, unburdened by the past, with a new family to take care of. She and Keelin were firm allies and friends.

Gianni and Piero got out on the level that housed his and Keelin's offices. People were packing up to leave for the end of the day and everyone cooed predictably as soon as they saw Piero, who lapped up the attention with a grin, but then he wriggled out of Gianni's arms so that he could go and play with one of his favourite security guards.

Gianni said warningly as Piero climbed up onto the man's lap and dug something out of a pocket, 'Don't say I didn't warn you, Alfredo. If he breaks your phone again, on your head be it!'

Gianni was on his fifth phone in the space of as many months. Alfredo didn't look remotely concerned though as chubby, sticky hands commandeered his phone with dextrous ease.

Gianni just shook his head ruefully and made his way to his wife's office which was beside his own, his heart rate increasing as it always did just before he saw her. Her assistant, who had been the wedding planner, was leaving and said with a smile, 'The conference call is just about finished—go on in.'

He almost scowled at the implication that anyone could keep him out.

He went into the room silently and closed the door, resting back against it with arms folded, and drank in the sight of Keelin pacing back and forth, gesticulating passionately. His blood surged and his hungry gaze devoured her, from the top of her head where her hair was pulled back into a loose knot, over the ripe curves of her breasts and eight-months-pregnant belly, evident in the stretchy dress, and down to her bare legs and feet.

She saw him and faltered, her eyes widening, cheeks going a little pink. Her words became a bit breathier. 'Okay, guys, I think that's it for now. I'll have Allessandra send you the results from the survey on Monday.'

There was a chorus of goodbyes from the phone on the desk and then she turned to face her husband with a slow sexy smile, hands resting over her belly.

Gianni yanked his tie off as he prowled to-

wards her, everything in him reacting with a
primal beat to the sight of her and her big belly.
Filled with his seed, *their* child. A girl. Who Gianni was already head over heels in love with.

He got to Keelin and pulled her close, growl-
ing softly, 'You shouldn't be working so hard.'

She lifted her arms to wind them possessively
around his neck and groaned softly when his
hands dropped down her back and caressed her
buttocks. She said with mock petulance, 'I'm
hardly working too hard—you're supervising
my every move and only allowing me to work
four hours a day, and what else do you expect
me to do in Rome while we wait for the baby?
Shop?'

Gianni pulled back and looked at her with a
wry gleam in his eye. 'And to think that once
upon a time I thought that's all you would ever
do.'

Keelin smiled cheekily. 'Ah, but I got you
good, Giancarlo Delucca.'

He agreed happily. 'You certainly did.'

She frowned, then asked, 'Where's Piero?'

Gianni indicated with his head. 'Outside with
Alfredo.'

She winced. 'I'd better get Allessandra to
order a new phone on Monday.'

Gianni smiled and manoeuvered his wife over
towards the sofa, sitting down and pulling her

with him so she sat across his lap. She laughed. 'I'll crush you!'

But he was too busy pulling her mouth down to his and sealing their reunion with a passionate kiss. He figured that they had about a minute before a ball of electric energy came looking for them and Gianni didn't intend wasting a second of that time.

* * * * *

WELCOME TO

THE CHATSFIELD

Dear Ms Abby Green,

We are delighted that you have booked your rooms to stay at The Chatsfield. And because we pride ourselves on creating the most unique and bespoke services during your stay, we have a few questions that we'd like to ask.

What time will you be checking in? *3pm*

Will you be checking in alone? *Yes*

What morning paper would you like delivered?

Financial Times ☐ Hello ☑ InStyle ☐
The Guardian ☑ The Times ☐

We would like to arrange some music for your listening pleasure. Is there a particular album or selection of music you would like to listen to in your room during your stay?

1. *Ellie Goulding*
2. *The Gloaming*
3. *London Grammar*
4.
5.
6.
7.

As we know that you may be working during your stay, we are aware of how important it is for you to have all your creature comforts around you. In order to ensure that your stay is as fulfilling as possible…

We have a wide selection of food available for room service delivery. What would be the most decadent meal that you would have delivered and why?

I would have very plain but beautifully cooked pasta with pesto sauce and a glass of white wine. I'm a cheap date!

Do you have any special requests for your stay at our hotel?

No disturbance in the morning. I like a quiet lie-in to read. ;)

What is your worst habit when writing?

Messing about on the internet.

Do you have a writing routine? If so, could you share a bit about it with us?

Start early before the distractions of the day creep in.

We're always looking to expand the Chatsfield library and welcome recommendations. What are the last two books you read and why?

I'm currently working my way through Diana Gabaldon's Outlander series and just finished A Breath of Snow and Ashes, Book 6. Now I'm reading An Echo in the Bone. I LOVE the love story between Claire and Jamie Fraser, and the whole complex world that Gabaldon has built around them. I could keep reading and re-reading them.

If you could write anywhere in the world, where would it be?

A little white-washed cottage in Greece by the sea on one of the islands.

We can tell from your recently published book that you have a vested interest in our very own hotels! So (curious minds want to know!) are you Team Chatsfield or Team Harrington?!

Well, in this book I'm Team Harrington at the start and then I switch to Team Chatsfield. Very fickle of me...

What did you most love about writing this story?

I loved how my heroine does her best to repel the hero.

What has been your best hotel experience and what made it memorable?

My best hotel experience was when a boss paid for me and my best friend to stay at the Beverly Hills Hotel in LA, and we were picked up and taken there from the airport in a chauffeur-driven limousine.

What has been your most unusual hotel experience and why?

Most unusual experience would have to have been in a hotel in Belfast when all the lights went out one night. It wouldn't have been so bad if I hadn't just been to the cinema to see The Blair Witch Project!

If you could have given your hero or heroine a piece of advice before they started on their journey in your story, what would it have been?

Hero: Look beneath the surface.

Heroine: Don't underestimate your enemy.

Thank you for answering our questions.

We very much hope you enjoy your stay!

WELCOME TO

THE CHATSFIELD

Dear Giancarlo Delucca,

To ensure that your stay at The Chatsfield is as exclusive and private as possible, we will need to ask you a few questions of perhaps a delicate nature, to ensure that our private security team will be best placed to support you.

If you had to pick your most public scandalous moment, what would it be?

I don't have any personal scandals, my main aim in life is to avoid that at all costs.

Was there an even more scandalous event that didn't make it into the press?

No.

What is your biggest secret?

That my father was in the Mafia and that I might be like him, rough and raw.

What do you love most about Keelin?

She drove me so crazy that I didn't even notice I'd fallen for her. Witch. I love her spirit and her bravery, and integrity.

What were your first thoughts when you saw you Keelin?

Not my type at all!

If your house were on fire and you could only save one thing, what would it be?

Nothing is as important as making sure my wife and family are safe.

What is the naughtiest thing you did at school?

Didn't you read the first answer?

What is your guiltiest pleasure?

Locking myself and my wife away in our villa in Umbria for a week with no one else there.

What is your worst habit?

I can be a little domineering. According to my wife.

What is your favourite film?

Ice Age 2. *(*coughs* My son's favourite film.)*

What present would you put beneath the Christmas tree for Keelin?

An eternity ring to remind her that she's mine, forever, just as I am hers.

How will you spend your first anniversary as a couple?

In bed. Doesn't matter where.

Thank you for your candour. We will endeavour
to ensure a scandal-free time during
your stay with us!

Mills & Boon welcomes you to the world of

THE
CHATSFIELD

Synonymous with style, spectacle…and scandal!

If you enjoyed this book, we know you'll love
the next book in the series.

Read on for an exclusive extract from
Carol Marinelli's thrilling instalment
in this exciting series:

PRINCESS'S SECRET BABY

'I am going to raise my baby alone.'

'Our baby,' James corrected, and Leila felt her throat constrict when she heard the snap of possession in his voice.

'I don't need your help in this, James.'

'It's not about what *you* need. It's about what the baby needs,' James said. 'Though I'd suggest that you do need some help. I've heard on the grapevine that your credit card has been stopped. I guess Mommy and Daddy are not very amused with their daughter's behaviour.'

'I don't think that they will ever speak with me again,' Leila said, 'so I doubt I will find out.'

James looked at her and felt a bit bad then—his parents were trouble enough, but Leila was dealing with a king and queen. 'I'm sure they'll come around.'

He took a breath; a sense of disquiet was growing as the ramifications of that thought hit home. Yes, her parents would surely come around and what then?

What happened then to the princess and her

baby?

What happened to *his* child?

'How did your parents take the news?' Leila asked.

'I'm not here to talk about our families,' James said. 'I'm here to sort things out between us.'

'There is no us,' Leila said.

'Who's your OB?' James asked, and she frowned. 'Your physician? You have seen someone other than the hotel doctor?'

'No.'

'You haven't had an ultrasound?' James checked, and she simply stared back at him. 'It might be twins!'

'There are a lot of twins in my family.'

The day just got better and better!

'So, Leila, what are you going to do for money now that your parents have cut you off?' James asked, and glanced around the room. He'd seen in the bedroom when he'd stood from the chair that her once-empty wardrobe was now bulging and there was a lot of evidence of her extravagance here too—she must have fifty bottles of perfume laid out on the table and the diamonds sparkling from her ears hadn't been there that night.

Her make-up was amazing though—her lips were in a neutral shade much more subtly seductive than that terrible red lipstick she had worn, and the touch of mascara she wore now accentuated the gold of her eyes.

'What I do for money is not your concern.'

'Actually, it is,' came James's sarcastic response, 'because, given the news, you're no doubt entitled to half of mine…'

'James,' Leila interrupted. 'I know there are laws here, that you will feel obligated, but I told you, I have already decided to go it alone. Anyway, I don't want someone so promiscuous or reckless as a father…'

'Don't. You. Dare!'

Leila shivered as she heard James, the man who had once made her smile, now speak in ice. The man whose voice had once soothed her now made her stomach clench.

'Don't you dare try to exclude me from my child's life. I'm not one of your servants that you can dismiss.'

'Actually,' Leila coolly said, and James's mouth gaped, 'you are.'

She got up and walked over to the table. She picked up the newspaper and tossed it to him, and then she opened a drawer and took out some magazines she'd spent a lot of time crying over and she tossed them at him too.

Then Leila picked up the phone and dialled three.

'I would like James Chatsfield removed now.'

'Tell them that I'm already leaving,' James said, and stood. He was struggling to stay calm. She was like no one he had ever dealt with, but there was no way that he'd let her simply remove him from his own child's life.

'I will call you later, Leila,' James said. 'And I very much suggest that you pick up the phone.'

As he went to walk away, something shot past him and James watched as a stiletto met with the wall as Leila vented some of her fury towards the man who had walked out on her that morning. The man who had left her pregnant with his child.

'Were they any good, James?' Leila shouted. 'Did even one of them come close to us?'

James said nothing. He wrenched open the door and was met with security. 'Just in time,' James quipped. 'You can escort me down.'

He got back to his penthouse and paced, his mind racing.

'Well, well.' Muriel, his daily, who was busy unpacking James's stuff from his trip to France, smiled.

'Well, well,' James said.

He liked Muriel. She was ancient and went about her business noisily, but was very possibly the one woman whose constant chatter didn't annoy him.

He flicked through his post that had gathered while he was away as Muriel chatted on.

'More money for me though,' Muriel said, as she fixed him a coffee. 'Those sticky fingers…'

'It won't be living here.' James grinned.

'What, you won't bring *it* here on your access visits?' Muriel said, handing him coffee. 'Are you going to walk *it* around the park for a few hours once a week?' She gestured her head to the delicious view of Central Park. 'It would be a bit cold in winter.'

He hadn't thought that far; all he'd thought was that he didn't want Leila leaving the country.

'I'll see it when I visit, Leila,' James said.

'Oh, my ex used to think he could just pop

around whenever he wanted,' Muriel said. 'I soon put him right.'

'I bet you did.' James laughed, but when Muriel had gone, he walked around his home, his absolute haven. A child? Here?

A baby!

He opened a spare bedroom that he was about to turn into a home theatre and he could not picture a baby in there, screaming its way through the night and wanting its mother.

He'd hire a nanny, James decided.

But Muriel had unsettled him. He was actually starting to think this through. By morning he had realised that she could leave at any moment, and with that thought he picked up the phone and was thankfully put straight through without The Harrington's usual games.

'I want you to move over to The Chatsfield,' James said. It was the only thing he could think of—at least that way he'd know if she checked out or if her family arrived to collect her.

'Why would I move there when I can stay here?'

'Leila,' James sighed. 'You can't afford to stay at The Harrington. And let me assure you Isabelle's charity will come at a price—she's not running a refuge for single moms. Don't for a minute think her offer came from the goodness of her heart. She's doing this to dirty my family's name.'

'You manage that by yourself,' Leila responded. 'I'm not leaving here.'

'Leila, I'm not asking you to move into my

home. I think this is an excellent idea. I'll have a suite arranged for you and I'll send a car to collect you at around lunchtime.'

'I have plans for lunchtime.'

God, she tested his patience to the limit. 'Tonight then,' James said, refusing to budge on this. 'I'll send my driver to collect you at eight.'

'I'm not moving out.'

'Will you at least agree to discuss it over dinner?'

'I don't want to have dinner with you. I don't want anything to do with you, James.'

'You should have thought about that three months ago,' James responded. 'Like it or not, we have to communicate. I can call my lawyer and get discussions started or you can meet me tonight and we can try to work things out ourselves.'

'I will only meet with you in the restaurant.'

'Fine,' James reluctantly conceded. 'We'll discuss our private business with half of the hotel watching on. Can you at least try and keep your shoes on this time?'

He ended the call and looked out to Central Park. The view sometimes soothed him, but it didn't today.

She'd leave, in his bones he was sure of it, and there was not a thing he could do once she was gone.

He'd marry her, James decided, even if he'd run from the very idea all of his life.

As if she'd agree though, James admitted to himself. He could barely get Leila to agree to dinner without threatening her with a lawyer.

A sudden thought occurred and again he found

himself on the phone to Manu, who was completely appalled at the idea he had just had and said that she would have no part in its execution.

'You can't force her to marry you, James, that's not fair.'

'She's pregnant with my child and could leave the country at any moment,' James clipped. 'I don't have time to be fair.'

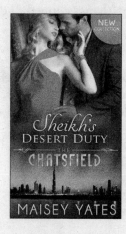